Designs on Her

Lake Chelan Book 2

To Misty!
Thanks for
joining the Romance
Writers Gone Wild
Party!

Enjoy!
Shirley Penick

SHIRLEY PENICK

Cover Photography by Wander Aquiar

Cover models: Amanda Renee and Scott Nova

Cover design and formatting by Cassy Roop of Pink Ink Designs

Editing by Deelylah Mullin

Contact me:

www.shirleypenick.com

www.facebook.com/ShirleyPenickAuthor

To sign up for Shirley's New Release Newsletter, send email to shirleypenick@outlook.com, subject newsletter.

Previous books by Shirley Penick

The Rancher's Lady: A Lake Chelan novella
Hank and Ellen's story

Sawdust and Satin: Lake Chelan 1
Chris and Barbara's story

Dedication

To my best buddy since junior high, Kathy Anderson, metalsmith and jewelry designer extraordinaire. Who endured many, many questions about the jewelry design business (any errors in the book are mine not hers). And who has made me my very own custom designed jewelry, that I love. To see all her beautiful work, search on Golden Ram Metalsmithing.

And as always, to my family and friends who support me continually and offer up brilliant suggestions when my brain gets tired and can't think.

Designs on Her

Chapter One

NOLAN THOMPSON WHIPPED into the yard in his patrol car. *Damn, people still here.*

"Dispatch, I'm at the Mathews' place. Two vehicles fully loaded, but not evacuated. I'll get them out of here."

"Ten-four, Officer Thompson. Probably the tanks she needs help with."

The back door on the truck was open and there was a very fine rear end sticking out from the backseat. He'd like to paddle that rear end. The fire was getting too close; he could smell the smoke even with the windows rolled up and a thick haze filled the yard. *Why hasn't this crazy woman evacuated?* He glanced around. There was an Airedale dog tied on the back porch. It looked like she'd done everything else right to prepare. She had a large firebreak dug between her house and the forest.

Hoses poured out water—although they weren't aimed at the house, but at a large shed. Her truck was parked close to the same structure. He stepped out of the squad car and slammed the door. She turned out of the vehicle and Nolan had to change his question to why hadn't this beautiful, crazy woman evacuated yet?

She said, "Thank God." Which he heard even over the roar of the flames. He didn't feel any heat from it, so it was still a safe distance away, but that could change in an instant.

"Ma'am you need to get out of here right now, the fire is heading this way."

"Kristen, call me Kristen—and yes, I know," she said and started dragging him by the arm toward the shed.

Nolan dug in his heels and said, "Did you get your household gas tanks loaded?"

"Yes, but—"

"Ma'am we really don't have time—"

Just then, one of the hotshot fire jumpers ran into the yard. "We've got to get this place evacuated now."

"Oh, two! Hallelujah!" the crazy woman said, grabbed hold of the firefighter, and started dragging them both toward the shed.

The fireman said, "Ma'am just what is it in that building that's so important to risk your life over?"

"I'm Kristen. The tanks."

Nolan said, "But you told me they were loaded."

"The household tanks, yes…" —she shoved both of them through the door to the structure— "but not those."

"Oh shit," the men said in unison. There, standing next to the door, were over a half dozen four-foot acetylene tanks.

"I can't carry them by myself or even with Mary Ann. They're too heavy," she said, pointing to the other woman in the room. "We got them to the doors by rocking them, but…."

The firefighter touched his mic and said, "Chief this is Trey, at the house on the ridge. I need another couple of guys over here stat, and have them bring at least two fire blankets."

"I was just sending them out. Is this an emergency?"

"The biggest one we've got right now. I'll explain later."

"Affirmative."

The men started carrying out the tanks and laying them in the cradles—which neither had noticed in the truck bed. Two other hotshots ran into the yard and over to the building. When they looked inside, one of them said, "Oh fuck, over a half dozen A5s."

The other one said, "Thank you, Lord, for this woman refusing to leave these behind."

The four guys made quick work of loading the acetylene. Just as they got the last one in, and the firefighters were securing them, a truck roared into the yard, and four men jumped out, running over to help. Three of them ran into the shed and started hauling out everything they could, to fill their truck. The firefighters joined them, helping to evacuate as much as possible.

Stoic, beautiful Kristen burst into tears and ran into

the arms of one of the men. She was babbling, "Oh, Chris, you came. I was so scared. You came, thank God. We couldn't lift them. They're too heavy. And the ground's too uneven. You came."

Chris stroked her hair saying, "It's okay, baby. I'm so sorry you were scared. Now, calm down and let's get the hell off this mountain pretending to be a volcano."

Kristen laughed and nodded.

"I'll drive your truck," Chris said.

Nolan, who felt a prick of disappointment that she had a boyfriend, said, "I'm going to ride with you, just in case we need two men for something. I need someone to drive the cruiser down."

Chris said, "Good. Terry can drive it. He's the mayor's son, so no worries."

"Perfect." While Nolan radioed into headquarters to notify them of the plan, Chris continued to bark out orders.

"Greg, go with Mary Ann. Kyle, drive my truck and take Farley with you—he's tied up on the back porch. Terry, take the squad car and try not to act like a kid in it. Hotshots, we owe you for saving one of our own."

"Shit man," Trey said, "she saved our ass by not leaving these here."

Greg nodded. "Still, come into my bar—when you get a chance. On the house."

Kristen was finally calm enough to speak. "Trey, use the house if you can, there's food and beds and water—no electricity or gas, but please feel free."

"Thanks, Kristen." The hotshots saluted and ran off toward the inferno.

The rest of them piled into the vehicles with Terry leading the way. Running lights and siren, they hauled ass down the mountain.

Once they were a safe distance from the fire Chris said, "Barbara is going to kick my ass for not getting up here sooner. I'm so sorry."

"Who's Barbara?" Nolan asked.

"My wife."

At the same time, Kristen said, "My sister."

"Oh," Nolan said, with an internal smile. Maybe she wasn't taken after all. Not that he had time for a woman—he was trying to make his mark in a new town and with his new job.

"What took you so long?" she asked.

"Being a dumbass! We were all just busy, trying to get everything ready for evacuation. The barge radioed in and said they were on their way. I didn't know anyone had called them yet, so when Kyle pulled in I assumed it was him, but he said no. Then it hit all four of us at the same time, that it must have been you. We knew you had to have help with the big tanks, so we burned rubber and ran lights and siren getting out of town and up the mountain. Why didn't you call one of us?"

"As soon as I hung up from calling the barge, I lost all communication and electricity. No cell, no landline, no radio. Apparently, I hadn't used the radio in such a long time the batteries had gone dead. So, I just started hauling out the household tanks and prayed like crazy that you guys would get up here in time. Then, I dug the fire break. Mary Ann showed up about the time I finished that, so we tried moving the big tanks and we did get them close to the door, but we couldn't lift them. I got the hoses started, pouring water over the shed. Then we boxed up the metals and gems to take in my truck and loaded her car up with clothes and stuff. When you still weren't here I tried to get Mary Ann to leave, but she wouldn't. So, we just kept boxing up more stuff."

"Damn, I'm sorry Kristen. You had to be scared." Chris placed his hand on her arm.

"I was terrified. I just got that load of acetylene last month. All six tanks are full, if the fire got to them—"

Nolan interrupted, "You didn't show it."

"I felt like bawling when you drove up, because I figured the three of us could move those hundred and eighty pound tanks. There wasn't time for hysterics."

Nolan said to Chris, "She was awesome. When I showed up trying to get her out, she just dragged me toward the shed. Then the first hotshot, Trey, came running in and she dragged us both toward the shed. She was cool as a cucumber, until they were loaded, and you drove in."

"Yeah, that's our Kristen, totally in control until the danger has passed, then she freaks out." Chris nodded.

"Hey," Kristen said.

"Am I lying?"

"No, but still, you don't have to tell everyone."

Nolan turned toward Kristen. Her long, straight brown hair was up in a crooked ponytail, she had dirt on her cheek, her big brown eyes were red and puffy from crying, her clothes were filthy, her hands were covered in grime, her fingernails torn and ragged. He laughed to himself, because he thought she was the most beautiful woman he had ever seen.

He said, "I'm Nolan Thompson, by the way. The new cop in town."

Kristen shook his outstretched hand. "Kristen Matthews, jewelry designer and currently a filthy, hot mess. Nice to meet you."

Nolan smiled and said, "A beautiful, hot mess, maybe. Jewelry designer, huh? I wondered what you had all those tanks for."

"Kyle, who does metal work, and I always split an order. The gas company requires orders of a dozen due to the fact we are so remote, and they have to be put on the barge to get here. These will last me a year or two providing they don't explode and kill everyone within a forty-mile radius."

"So, you plan to put them on the barge and then what?" Nolan asked.

"The barge will take them across Lake Chelan and put them on the other side in a large storage structure. It was built when I was a kid, and we had a huge forest fire between us and Chelan. It's large enough to evacuate most of the town. I don't think we're quite there yet, but those of us who live on the mountain and also people like Kyle and myself who have large amounts of flammable gas, can put those over there for safety. Some of the in-town people might want to put valuables over there or things that need extra time to evacuate."

"Good. Nice to know the town has plans in place for emergencies like this."

"Since I had all that time to load up, I brought most of my stuff down. Mary Ann's car is full and my truck and now your truck Chris. I don't know what to do with all of it, but I'm glad it won't burn up if the hotshots lose control up there."

"You can stay with us," Chris said.

"I know. And I will for a day or two, but you know how long these things rage on. It could be a couple of months—even up to the first snow. I'll probably see if Kyle has anything I can rent. I have some orders I need to keep working on. So, if I can find a place to set up shop, that would be better."

Chris's green eyes sparkled. "I think the guys got nearly everything out of your workroom, so you should have everything you need."

"Looks like we made it safe and sound," Nolan said with relief, as they turned the corner into town.

Kristen smiled at him. "Well, you've had quite an introduction to our town, Officer Thompson. Kind of a trial-by-fire."

Nolan laughed out loud. "Good one. I can hardly wait to see what's next."

Chapter Two

KRISTEN WAS HAPPY TO SEE most of her acetylene loaded onto the ferry. She had been scared to death those tense hours waiting for someone to arrive to help her. She'd worked like a dog to get it all ready as the fire crept closer. She had actually been able to taste the smoke *and her fear*—and that combination was not good. She really needed to figure out a way to be more self-sufficient with those damn tanks. She'd seen some motorized tank movers which would be good if the ground was level and she had a ramp to get them on the truck. She'd look into it for the future—maybe pour some concrete, make a mini loading dock. For today she was safe. She'd never been so frickin' glad to see a man in her whole life when that cop showed up.

Nolan Thompson was going to have a hero's place in

her heart for a while. Of course, the man was also gorgeous. He had to be six foot four and looked strong as an ox. His uniform fit him just right. Dark brown hair and—once he had taken off his sunglasses—bright blue eyes. Nice to have a good-looking guy to see once in a while, since she wasn't really interested in having a man in her life. They were unreliable and a pain in the ass. *But eye candy. I can enjoy that as well as any woman.*

Chris came up and put his arm around her neck. "Let's go see your sister, she's probably worried and that's not good for the baby."

Kristen rolled her eyes at him. This was their first child even though they had been married for ten years. Her sister had mellowed out a lot in the last few months and had finally wanted to have kids. So, now she was pregnant and her husband, Chris—who used to be laid back—was a little on the crazed side about the baby.

"Alright, worry wart. We can go check in with prego woman."

Chris grinned at her, not in the least repentant about his hovering.

"Oh, wait. Let me ask Kyle about rentals."

"I already put a bug in his ear about you wanting one. He said he'd look through his listings to see if anything had an outbuilding where you could set up your work area."

Kristen nodded. "Perfect. Let's go see my sister, then."

"My wife. The mother of my unborn baby."

She grinned. "Okay, you win. Meet you there. House or shop?"

"Shop."

Kristen pulled her truck around the back of Barbara's wedding and costume shop, got Farley out of the front seat, and tied him up outside in the shade with some water in his bowl. Then, she went in the rear entrance. Christa, one of her sister's partners, was in the kitchen. "Hi, Christa, how's it going?"

"Oh, it's good to see you, Kristen. I take it you got evacuated."

"Yep, safe and sound. Hopefully, my house will stay that way. All of my work stuff is in the truck, so I can still get some things done—if I find a good place to setup."

"These fires are really bad this summer. Worse than they've been in years."

"Yeah, I remember them being bad when I was in elementary school, but not too much since then."

Chris came in and kissed Christa on the cheek. "Hi, how's the little woman?"

"She's good, Chris. Upstairs working on a new design, I think. We've got a bride in Cleveland wanting something special. Barbara's been trying to come up with something, but the bride shoots her down every time. She might be a bridezilla in disguise."

"Oh, no. Let's go see if we can distract her, Kristen."

"Coming right after you; just want to check with Christa on my jewelry. Oh, and maybe wash my hands and face. I'll need to change clothes, but that can wait."

Christa smiled. "We could use a couple of pieces— come look at the display case and see what you think."

"You're right, you've got some holes. Those pieces with the blue stones just run out of here, don't they?"

"I think the brides like the idea of wearing a blue piece of jewelry for their *something blue*."

"Sure looks that way. I'll get some more pieces made up for you."

"Thanks."

Kristen walked into her sister's workroom office in time to hear Barbara screech, "You didn't remember about my sister? Chris!"

"It's okay. Calm down, little sis, I'm fine. A very hot cop showed up—and between him and the cute firefighter, they got all my tanks in the truck."

"But, Chris, how could you forget my sister!" She burst into tears, jumped up, ran into the bathroom, and slammed the door.

"Barbara…" Kristen started to say.

Chris just shook his head and whispered, "Hormones. She does this every day. Don't worry, it doesn't last long."

"Every day?"

"Every. Day."

"Better you than me, my friend. I don't think I could deal with that every day."

"The first few times it happened I freaked out. Then one day, Mrs. Erickson motioned me over to her house and sat me down. She told me it was going to be just fine and we had quite the conversation about pregnancy and hormones. I've been taking it better ever since."

"That snoopy, old lady that lives across the street? Our third-grade teacher?" Kristen asked.

"The very one. She heard the hysterics, since it's summer and the windows are all open. She's saved my bacon more than once—so if the woman has something she wants to tell me, I go over and drink tea and eat cookies and listen to every word she has to say."

Kristen laughed. "Okay, then. Good for you."

Barbara came out of the bathroom perfectly calm and grabbed a chocolate chip cookie out of the container on her desk. "Hi, Kristen. Would you like to come stay with us while the fire is up around your house?" She took a big bite of the treat.

Kristen gave Chris a WTF look and he just shrugged.

"Maybe for a few days. I hope Kyle will be able to find me a place to rent. I need to set up my workbench—it takes a lot of space and it needs to be unattached from the house."

"Of course. Do you have a lot of pieces you're working on?" Barbara said around a mouthful of cookie.

"Yeah, Vangie bought a bunch of cabs, in an auction so she's got lots of things for me to work on." At Chris's confused expression she said, "Cabs are cabochons to you rookies or you probably would call them stones. Anyway Barb, I've got all that for Vangie and then your shop could use a few new pieces and—"

Barbara interrupted, crumbs flying. "Oh, I know! The building next door is empty—it's a Victorian like mine. It has a retail space below and living quarters above—but the best part is, it has an awesome studio in the huge garage."

"Is it for rent? I don't really want a retail space, but the rest sounds good."

"I think it's for sale actually," Chris interjected.

"Oh, I don't want to buy anything."

Barbara said, "You could always ask Kyle about it. Although, if you did buy it, once you move back up the mountain you could let someone rent it. It's worth looking into. It would be fun to have you right next door for a few weeks—until they get the fire under control. Let's go look in the windows," she said standing up and dropping the half-eaten cookie on her desk.

"I think we should call Kyle and have him bring over the keys."

"Oh, Chris. You are such a party pooper." Barbara crossed her arms and narrowed her eyes at him.

Chris kissed her on the forehead. "Anyway, I probably should get back to the amusement park. It amazes me how people are still coming in droves even though we've got a fire raging on the mountain."

"Okay, honey. You have a good day."

Kristen glared at him sending the silent message, *I can't believe you're leaving me with the crazy one.*

Chris smirked and walked out the door.

Barbara said, "So, let's call Kyle and see what he says."

"We can do that. All my tools and work paraphernalia is in the truck. I don't want to leave it in there too long, so finding a place quickly would be good."

While Barbara called Kyle, Kristen looked out the window to check on Farley. He was happy as could be in the backyard shade. She shifted her view toward the property Barbara had suggested—and from her perspective out the window, it did look nice. The building in the back appeared large and it had lots of windows and skylights.

"Kyle will be by an a few minutes. He said the owners aren't really interested in renting—but they are highly motivated to sell, so it would be a steal."

"But buying something in town just seems weird."

"With the town starting to turn around—economy-wise—because of the amusement park and some of the other plans, it really might be a good time to buy. You might be able to turn it for a tidy profit in a year or so."

"Maybe you should buy it then," Kristen snarked.

"No can do. We've pretty much gotten our finances stretched with taking my online wedding dress business and expanding it to this boutique. We bought this building a couple of months ago—when I brought Christa and the others on as partners. And then Chris doing the amusement park full time—even with Gus's backing—it's not a good time for us. Especially with the baby coming."

"Yeah, that's probably true. I'll take a look at it. But I really don't think I want to buy something." Kristen heard her stomach rumble. "I'm going to get some clean clothes and see if you have anything I can steal in the fridge. I'm starved."

"Help yourself."

Kristen grabbed a cookie and went out to her truck to

get some clean clothes while they waited for Kyle. Once she was refreshed she looked in the fridge and saw some Cokes. She grabbed one and downed it. And not a diet soda—she needed sugar. All that work this morning had her faint from hunger; the sugar and caffeine hit her with a jolt. The Coke burned her throat as she swallowed. *The smoke must have made it raw.* She saw some cheese and took a few pieces and some crackers. That would tide her over for a while.

Kristen heard the door open and saw Kyle.

She went with Barbara and Kyle over to see the house. Barbara gushed over the retail space and the upstairs living area.

Kristen did think it was nice, but she couldn't see what she'd do with the retail space. The living area was lovely—it had three bedrooms with renovated bathrooms, a family room, and a full kitchen. The apartment had both an internal staircase from the retail area as well as an outdoor entrance. So, if she did want to do something with the downstairs she wouldn't have to go through it to get in and out of the living space. Still, it was nicely done, but nothing to write home about.

Until she got to the studio. That was awesome. It was so well lit, with a lot of natural light and plenty of space. She could really see herself working in that space and it nearly made her drool. Kyle was a very good realtor and he noticed her marked interest in the workroom. So, that's where they talked cost. It was a really good price—the people who owned it had retired and moved to Phoenix, so they just wanted to get it sold and out of their hair. They were willing to hold the loan if needed. Kristen was a good businesswoman and she knew what her finances looked like, so when Kyle quoted her the monthly payment she knew she could afford it.

Her house on the mountain was paid off and she had good insurance, so even if it burned she'd be able to replace it without too much trouble. She lived a pretty quiet lifestyle, so all her money had gone to building her sales, and the guys had loaded everything that wasn't nailed down into Chris's truck. She really wouldn't lose anything of value if she was unfortunate enough to lose her home—which was a possibility—so, maybe it would be good if she bought this place in town. That way, she could keep working even if she had to rebuild after the fire.

"All right, let's do it. Make an offer and draw up the papers. I think I'd rather go with a conventional loan, so see if they would take another twenty thousand off for not carrying the loan. And, I don't want to wait forever to move in, see what kind of magic you can come up with, Kyle. Maybe I could rent it while the paperwork goes through."

Kyle smiled. "I'll get right on it. They might not want to rent, but they might let you move in with some earnest money."

"It will be so much fun having you right next door." Barbara laughed and clapped her hands.

Chapter Three

THREE DAYS LATER, Kristen was setting up her workbench in the lovely studio next to Barbara's shop. The owners had accepted her offer with an unusually small amount of haggling, and Kyle had worked with her earnest money to get her an early move in date. The loan had been applied for, so everything was coming along. She got a few pieces of furniture for the living space—just a bed, a couch and a kitchen table. The stove and fridge had been left; they worked but were nothing special. Once she closed she'd think about more permanent furnishings.

Chris and his friends helped her move in, so it didn't take long. She only had one half-full acetylene tank since the rest were across the lake. The inferno was still raging on the mountain but it wasn't coming any closer to town. The hotshots up on the mountain and the volunteer firefighters from town were both keeping a close eye on the firebreak.

Kristen was happily setting up her work area and was relieved to be able to have her own space. It was great to be able to stay with her sister, but the pregnancy hormones made Barbara a little on the crazy side. She always had strong emotions, but these were over-the-top and three days was *more* than enough time in the same house. But more importantly, Kristen needed to work. She didn't do idle—she liked to keep busy and she needed to create. On top of that, she also had deadlines. She could move them, of course, but she didn't want to, unless she really had no choice in the matter.

This new studio was much larger than her shed on the mountain and the light was incredible. It had previously been a painter's workspace and she could still smell a hint of turpentine and oil paints. It would soon be smelling like flux, metal, and acetylene. The guys had packed more into Chris's truck than she realized. She didn't think there was much—if anything—left up by the fire.

The knock on the door startled her. She wasn't used to people interrupting when she was working. Mary Ann was supposed to come over later this afternoon.

At the door was the hot cop with the wild blue eyes. "Well, hello, officer. Welcome to my new studio."

"Hello, Ms. Matthews. I heard you were purchasing this property and thought I'd stop by to see if you needed any help—with the tanks or whatever."

"That's nice of you, but most of my tanks are still on the

other side of the lake and Chris and the other guys from town gave me a hand this morning. But you're welcome to come in and take a look at my new amazing workspace."

"Thanks." He came in the door and looked around. "I have to say this is an awesome room. So much light—and it has a nice open feel to it. Should be easy to create in a space like this."

"Now, Officer Thompson, you sound like a man who knows his way around a studio. Do you have a secret life that no one has managed to find out about? And you can call me Kristen. Ms. Matthews makes me think of my mother."

"I'll call you Kristen if you will call me Nolan. And no I don't have a secret life, but I do have a glass artist for a mother and I spent a lot of time in her workroom."

Hmm. Glass artist. Thompson. Lightbulb moment. "You aren't talking about Lucille Thompson, are you? Her art is amazing."

"The very one."

"Oh, my. Well, I had no idea I was in such elite company. I studied your mother when I was in college. I remember reading an article that mentioned a son. I think she called him Little Guy, is that you?"

Nolan's ears turned red. "Yes, that's me, but I'd prefer Nolan if it's all the same to you."

Kristen laughed. "I imagine Little Guy isn't so appropriate anymore. You must be six-four."

"Good guess. So, yeah. I now tower over my five-foot six-inch mother."

"So do you have any artistic talents that you either hide or ignore?"

"My mother did teach me the craft and I can handle the mechanics just fine, but the inspiration and design aren't there."

"Do you have the equipment to make glass art?"

"I do in a storage facility. It's not easy getting things into Chedwick and the kiln is heavy and bulky—even if it is a relatively small one. Now that I'm more settled I might have it boxed up and shipped—but I'm in no hurry, since I don't really have any driving desire to create."

"I do hope you have it shipped. I'd love to see how it all works."

"I'd love to see how you work—so maybe you could show me and I could show you."

"That almost sounds naughty. Were you one of those boys on the playground offering girls a peek?" Kristen gasped. *Oh, dear God.* Did she really say that? Her face heated. "Um, I mean, um damn, just ignore that."

Nolan chuckled. "Don't worry, Kristen. I'm not going to take offense. And let me just say that no, I wasn't one of those boys. However, in your case, I might be willing to make an exception."

"Oh, my." She looked into his blue eyes to see if he was kidding and saw nothing except maybe a little lust. When someone knocked on the door she nearly collapsed with relief. "I need to get that."

Nolan looked away. "I should probably go anyway."

"Whatever you want."

"Oh, it's definitely not what I want, but it might be best."

Kristen opened the door to find Mary Ann.

Nolan said goodbye to both of them and walked away.

Mary Ann watched him get into his car. "That was the cop that came up to your house, wasn't it?"

"Yes. Nolan Thompson."

"What did he want?"

"To see if I needed any help. I guess. Actually, I'm not quite sure."

"Hmm. On his day off, even."

"What?" Kristen asked.

"You didn't notice he was in jeans and driving his own car? Not a patrol car?"

"No, I guess I didn't notice."

"Okay, then. So, show me this studio you have been raving about for three days."

Mary Ann walked in and Kristen looked back to where she'd last seen Nolan get into his car. *His day off, huh. What did that mean?* She huffed and shut the door before she went to show Mary Ann her new space.

NOLAN DROVE OFF, both frustrated and relieved that Mary Ann had shown up. He had been going down a path he wasn't sure he was ready for, and by her non-reaction he decided Kristen probably wasn't ready for it yet, either. For

Pete's sake, he'd only met her three days ago and they had hardly talked then, being too busy avoiding a catastrophe. But that hadn't stopped him. He had been coming on to her and he wasn't sure she'd even noticed—she certainly didn't return any interest. He really needed to get a grip.

Maybe he could bring her some dinner later. After spending all day moving, she might appreciate that. Something from Amber's or maybe some cookies or pie from Samantha's bakery.

Damn, he was doing it again. *I have to stop this nonsense right now—before I turn into a stalker.* There were a lot of pretty ladies in town. Why was he so obsessed with this one? Some of the other women had clearly hit on him—a couple of times. *But no, I wasn't the least bit interested in any of those perfectly nice females. I have to go and be infatuated with the recluse that lives on the top of the mountain.*

He wasn't going back to her house tonight, at least that much he could be certain of.

Mary Ann gushed, "Oh, Kristen, you have to do something with this space. It's amazing. You should open a gallery—there are plenty of people that could put their artwork in here."

"No. I don't want a gallery. I don't want a retail space. I don't want a bunch of people tramping through my house."

"But you're going to be upstairs in the living area or out

in the studio. This retail space has been very thoughtfully designed. It has awesome lighting. Do you see how the lighting deliberately sets up areas of interest? If you took each area and focused on one particular artist it would be spectacular. Can't you just imagine Kyle's metal sculptures over in that larger area? And your jewelry would be fantastic on those pedestals of different heights. That area in the other room has a very playful attitude—it would be great to showcase the wooden toys Greg and Terry are making. Oh, and next to that you could put some of Jeremy's children's books."

"Stop. I don't want to envision it, because I don't want to do it. I need my solitude and I can't imagine having to deal with all those people, let alone tourists. No, no, no."

"You wouldn't have to do it; you could hire someone or—"

"And I don't want employees. Are you trying to kill me?"

"Okay, try not to have a breakdown. It was just an idea. A stellar idea, but I get it. I get you. It's okay. Breathe."

She took a deep breath. "All right, then. I'm not going to stress about this. Let's go upstairs and have some tea… or maybe vodka."

"A little too early in the day for vodka. A glass of wine might be good."

"I don't have any wine—or vodka, for that matter. But I do have tea."

Chapter Four

NOLAN JUST COULDN'T RESIST driving by Kristen's new place. It was like looking at a car wreck—he just had to see whatever he could see. He had been going by every day while *on patrol*. Did this street need patrolling that often? Hell no, it was a quiet street. It did have some businesses on it, but nothing crazy. Except for his favorite crazy woman—who was currently attempting to carry a huge box into her home. She would pick it up and walk three steps and then put it back down. Couldn't the woman ask for help, ever?

Nolan parked his patrol car in front of her house, called in that he'd be out of touch for a few minutes, and went over to where she'd moved the box another three steps.

"Um, do you want some help?"

She jumped. "Oh, you scared me. I was channeling my strength."

"Wouldn't it be easier to ask for some help?"

"I tried that, Mister Smarty Pants, and everyone was busy. They had a problem down at the amusement park with the carousel and everyone is over there fixing it. One of the animals came loose, or a foot fell off, or something. Anyway, Chris and Terry and Greg are all over there fixing it. Kyle is showing a house. Mary Ann is at the school this morning, doing her monthly volunteer thing. And I really didn't think I should ask my pregnant sister." Her voice got shriller with each word.

Nolan held up his hands in surrender. "Sorry, sorry, I jumped to a false conclusion. Please forgive me. And here, let me give you a hand."

"Gladly. This damn thing is heavier than it looked when I ordered it."

"And it's bulky which makes the heaviness even worse."

"Thanks, Einstein. I had no idea." Kristen snarked.

"Woah, you're having a bit of a bad day aren't you."

"Again, another brilliant observation. And if you say one word about PMS, I will punch you right in the nose."

"That wouldn't be a wise move. In case you haven't noticed, I have my uniform on and that would be assaulting an officer."

Kristen glared daggers at him and marched into the building. Damn, now he'd really done it. "Kristen wait, I'm sorry. How can I help? Come on, I really am sorry, give the poor stupid man a break, please. Pretty please, with sugar on top."

Kristen came back to the door. "Okay, since you asked so nicely. Let's just get this frickin' box in the house."

"Good. I'm going to tip it over so we can each grab an end."

He tipped it over and they got it into the house and up the stairs to her living quarters. When they got it into her front room and set down, she said, "Kitchen."

He followed her in where she took two cold water bottles out of the refrigerator and handed him one. He gladly drank half of it and sat across the table from where she'd collapsed.

"Thank you very much for stopping and giving me a hand with that. I never would have gotten it upstairs by myself."

"It scares me to think of you trying to get it up the stairs alone. Where's your dog?"

"Oh, he was trying to help and kept getting in the way so I tied him up out back with a rawhide bone and a bowl of water. Hey, how can you just take off from working? Don't you have to be on duty when you're, well, on duty?"

"I called in a lunch break. So, someone else will cover for me."

"Lunch," she said, jumping up. "You can't help me on your lunch hour, you'll be starving by the end of the day. Here, let me get food out, for a sandwich."

"It's okay, I'll be fine."

"No, I insist." And with that she started laying bread

and lunch meat and lettuce and mayo and mustard and cheese and carrots and soda and chips and fruit and cookies on the table. Then she got two plates and a couple of knives and put them next to the food.

"Wow, I can't eat all that."

"No, but I can help you," she said with a grin.

"Excellent." Everything she laid out looked good; he must be getting hungry.

Nolan started heaping everything on a sandwich and then he felt uncomfortable—was he making a pig of himself? —so he looked over at Kristen's sandwich. Hers had more stuff piled on than his did, that made him feel better. He finished stacking it on and then cut it in half and took a bag of chips and some carrots and celery.

Before he took a big bite he asked, "So what's in that box anyway?"

Kristen chewed her bite and when she'd swallowed said, "A dresser. I'm buying a few things to make it more comfortable here until the closing. After that, I feel like I can really get settled. At least for a few weeks, until I can go back up the mountain. Providing it doesn't burn down."

"What will you do with this place when you go back up? I refuse to believe the hotshots will let your place burn down. Besides, I noticed you had a good sized fire break dug."

"Yeah, well, I did try to do everything right. I don't really know what I will do with this place. Barbara convinced me that even if I move back up there, I could keep it for a while and turn it for a tidy profit as the town gets in better shape."

"Things do seem to be improving, at least from what people have said. Chris's idea to capitalize on the Tsilly Adventures game seems to have paid off. The amusement park looks very prosperous. I've heard he plans to expand it this winter."

"Yes, and maybe next winter too. We have some other plans too."

"Oh, what are those?"

"We want to showcase our artisans in an online joint web page, as well as a brochure that we can put into neighboring town hotels and restaurants. And Mayor Carol also wants to make this a wedding destination, she's planning on retiring next year and running a Bed and Breakfast to help."

"With the park, all you artisans, and the wedding destination that should breathe quite a bit of life back into the town."

"That's what we're all hoping for. We about went belly-up at the first of the year. Several business owners had talked to Mayor Carol about the probability of having to move this summer. But then, Chris got the amusement park going and some negative publicity worked in our favor, so we had a flood of people book vacations."

"Do you plan to do anything with the downstairs while you're here? From what I saw, it's a nice space. It might make a good gallery."

Kristen groaned. "Not you too! My sister has

mentioned it. My helper Mary Ann had it all but open, in her mind, and was pushing for it. She'd decided where each person's art would look the best. I'm really not much of a people person and I really don't want to run something like that."

"Why would you have to run it at all? Couldn't you just turn the whole thing over to Mary Ann? If she had it all planned out, why wouldn't she be the logical person?"

"She would be, of course, but I don't want to have any part of it."

"Would you really have to? Couldn't you just, like, rent her the space and lock the door here at the top of the stairs? It's got an outside entrance which would give you access to the studio and the garage for your car. Would you really need to be a part of it?"

"I just don't know if I could handle it all. There's a reason I live on the top of the mountain—away from everyone else."

"I understand. Don't let it stress you out. I was just playing devil's advocate. And now, I better get back to work. Lunch time is over and they are going to start wondering where I am. Thanks for the food."

"Thanks for helping me get the box up the stairs."

"My pleasure, feel free to ask for my help anytime. I love to help pretty ladies."

"Yeah, I'll call the dispatcher and tell her I have a box emergency at my home and please send only Officer Thompson."

He took her phone from the table and programmed his number into it. "There, no excuses."

She laughed. "Fine, but I probably won't call anyway."

"Now, what a surprise that is. Not. Hey, how do you plan to put that dresser together?"

"Um, with tools?"

"Smart alec. I'll be back after my shift and we can put it together, together. You can feed me again as payment or we could order a pizza."

"Okay. You have a deal. With that plan, I don't have to feel guilty about not working on it now and I can go to my studio. My nice, quiet, studio. With no people."

Nolan laughed. "See you later, then."

Chapter Five

KRISTEN DIDN'T GET TO HER studio quite as quickly as she'd planned. She wasn't going to feed the man pizza—especially after all the help he'd been to her. He was still at hero standing in her book, since he hadn't— yet—done something stupid to put him into pain-in-the-ass-man status, where she felt most men lived their lives. So, she wanted to feed her hero something good. Since she still didn't have a lot of groceries—other than sandwich makings—that meant begging some food off her sister.

Men almost always liked steaks and Chris had recently gotten a side of beef—from the butcher that processed Hank Jefferson's cattle. Steak, potatoes, the town's famous veggie recipe, and some kind of pie from Samantha's bakery would be perfect. *Hmm. Beer or wine?* Beer. She wasn't a big wine drinker and she could make some iced tea too. Sounded like a plan—now all she needed to do was gather the ingredients.

She saw her sister's car was next door at the boutique, so she went over into the back door and up the stairs—since Barbara hardly ever spent time in the shop. They were both pretty introverted, so they tended to stay in the background creating. She said hi to the other ladies as she passed them. Her sister had a good group of women working with her and they seemed to love both sewing and working in the showroom. So, it was a win-win for all four of them—which is why Barb had brought them on as partners. She'd decided about the same time that it was the right stage in her life to have a child.

She knocked once on the doorframe and walked into the office. Barbara was bent over her drafting table and Kristen knew not to interrupt until she stopped with whatever she was working on. Most women were multi-taskers, but not Barbara. She had a single-minded focus that sometimes bordered on obsession. It had caused some problems in her marriage a while back, but she and Chris had worked hard to get their relationship on track. Good communication had been the key.

Barbara put down her pencil and sat up, stretching her back. She moaned softly and turned to Kristen. "Hello sister of mine. I thought you would be hard at work in your awesome studio. What brings you to my domain?"

"I will be hard at work, as soon as I mooch some dinner fixings from you."

"Oh? Like what?" Her sister asked.

"A couple of steaks, and the ingredients for the veggies if you have them."

Barbara's eyebrows went up. "A couple of steaks? Who are you having over?"

"That new cop, Nolan Thompson. He saw me trying to get the dresser into the house and stopped by to lend a hand. He also offered to help me put it together if I fed him. Since it appears to have a million parts and an encyclopedia-sized instruction manual, I decided I was getting the better deal."

"Interesting," Barbara said with a knowing smile.

"Not interesting. Handy."

"Uh huh. And the fact that he's a hunk-and-a-half has nothing whatsoever to do with it."

"He *is* easy on the eyes, but I'm not really interested in anything," Kristen said firmly.

"Hell, it doesn't have to be anything permanent—but you *could* have a little fun with the guy. You know like a *man*-made orgasm or two."

"Kristen! You're married and pregnant."

"Yes, and how do you think I got this way?"

"Okay, I give. I don't need to hear details about my little sister's love life. That would just be TMI."

Barbara laughed. "Gotcha. Anyway, I'm not talking about the hottie cop for me, I'm talking about him for you. I already have my hands full with Chris, thank you very much."

"Hands and other places it seems."

"Ha! I thought you didn't want to go there, missy."

Kristen shuddered. "I don't. I really don't. So, about those steaks?"

"Of course. What's mine is yours. Steaks are on the far-left side in the big freezer. There are veggies and grated Swiss cheese in the fridge freezer, soup and fried onions in the pantry."

"Thanks sis. I'm going to run so I can get some work done today." Kristen kissed her sister on the cheek.

"Great. And if you get a chance and feel the urge, jump the man. Relieve some stress."

"No stress relief needed. 'Bye." And with that, she ran out the door and down the stairs.

"*Bwak, bwak,*" she heard Barbara call out.

Kristen was in her studio an hour later with the steaks and veggies thawing, the tea brewing, and a blueberry pie on the counter. She set her phone to go off at five-thirty so she wouldn't get caught up and forget to go start dinner. She was an artist after all.

NOLAN FINISHED HIS shift and headed home to shower and change out of his uniform. He wanted to go by the store on his way and see if there were some flowers or something he could take with him. It wasn't a date exactly, but he hated to show up empty-handed. He didn't know if she drank wine, and he wasn't ready to ask others about her preferences. Chocolate was always good, so if they didn't have any flowers at the tiny market they had in town that would be an option.

An hour later, Nolan pulled up to the house and looked at the passenger seat—he'd gone crazy in the store. He had flowers, chocolate, wine, and a pretty little picture of Lake Chelan. He'd clearly lost his mind and he was sure she'd think he was a nut. But he just didn't seem to be able to control himself. He could always leave some of it in the car—not the flowers, they had to go in. And the sun was still out, so, the chocolate would melt in the hot car and he didn't think it was a good idea to leave the wine in the sun, either. So, that left the picture of Lake Chelan—but it had reminded him of the view from her mountain top home, and he wondered if she missed it up there. Darn it, he wasn't going to leave any of it in the car. Nope, guess he'd just look like an idiot.

KRISTEN WAS A wreck. She was so damn nervous, she'd gone through every article of clothing she owned before she finally decided on some shorts and a tank top. She'd been tempted to wear a sun dress but they were going to be crawling around on the floor putting the dresser together, so that was a stupid idea. But shorts just didn't seem right. She was about to go back to her room to change into the dress anyway, when he knocked on the door. Too late— shorts it was going to be.

She answered the door and there he stood with his hands full. Flowers, candy, wine and something else. What the heck?

"I know, total overkill, but I just couldn't arrive empty-handed and when I stopped at that little tourist store in town I bought everything. I didn't know what you would like."

Kristen snickered, then she snorted and then she laughed out loud. "Thank God, you're as big of a mess as I am," she said between guffaws.

A grin slid slowly across Nolan's face. "Really? You too?"

"Oh yeah. I tried on every piece of clothing I owned—nothing seemed right. Almost went for a sundress. Which would have been interesting putting the dresser together, don't you think?"

"Let me say those shorts and top are just fine by me. You look awesome."

"So, what are all these gifts you have?"

"Pretty flowers for a pretty lady. Wine to have with dinner. Chocolate just because. And a picture of Lake Chelan that reminded me of your view from the top of the mountains, in case you were feeling homesick."

"Wow."

"Did I do okay then?"

"Oh yeah." She took everything from his hands and laid them on the counter. "And since you've got me all mushy let's just get this out of the way now." She grabbed him by the arms, pulled him in, and kissed him. He didn't react at first as she brushed her lips against his, but once he got on board with the idea, he took over and kissed her breathless. He tasted like sin, he smelled like some kind of manly soap, and she loved the feel of his hard frame up against her soft one. Her whole body tingled, her knees turned to jelly, and she got lightheaded.

When he finally drew back, she sucked in a deep breath. "Okay, then."

"Hmm, I was thinking more like *whooo hooo*! Damn, girl. You are one fine kisser."

"I was just along for the ride," Kristen said as Farley started barking.

"I sure hope you enjoyed it as much as I did."

"Maybe not as noisily as you, but yes. I did. Now let's see if we can get Farley calmed down and eat some dinner—before I burn it."

"Sounds good. And if I promise to be quieter, can I have a repeat?"

"We'll see."

Kristen put the food on the table and then turned to Nolan. "Do you want some of that wine you brought or a beer?"

"I guess I'd prefer a beer, but I'll have wine with you, if you want."

"Nope, I actually prefer beer. Not a huge wine drinker, but it's my sister's favorite, so I'll have it with her. Well, eventually. Since she's pregnant and not drinking. *Hmm*."

"No worries. Wine stays fine for nine months. This smells delicious."

"She's a few months along, so it won't be that long. Oh, except she's planning to nurse, so maybe it will be longer. Who knows about this kind of thing? This is the first baby in the family since she was born. So, I may be a little rusty on how this all goes. Or in reality, completely clueless."

Nolan laughed as he took up a fork of the vegetables. "I have several cousins with little kids, so maybe I can give you some pointers."

"We might need them."

"These vegetables are great. So, is it just you and your sister?"

"Yes. My dad ran off with a younger woman when Barbara and I were kids. He left us pretty much destitute, so mom worked her ass off trying to keep a roof over our head and food on the table. The fact that she worked at the restaurant helped with the food on the table, but wages in waitressing are pretty measly, so it wasn't easy. Mom died a few years ago. She got the flu and her body was so run down, from so many years of working like a dog, she couldn't fight it."

"Your mother died from the flu? Really?"

"Yeah, I didn't know that happened either—but they say it does in the elderly or people with a poor immune system. Mom was working too hard. Barbara was still launching her wedding dress business and I was trying to get my jewelry to pay the bills. She died shortly before the Tsilly Adventures game was released. I did a bunch of charms for the first thousand people who bought the game and that got me launched. But not in time to give mom a hand, so she could slow down. Timing sucks sometimes."

Nolan reached out and took her hand, rubbing his thumb across her knuckles. "Yeah, it does suck, sometimes."

"All right. Enough melancholy. Let's talk about something else."

"Right. *Hmm.* How about baby chicks and how cute and cuddly and soft and fuzzy they are?"

Kristen gaped at him. The man had lost his mind. Cute, cuddly chicks? Really? From the six-foot four mountain of a man? Fuzzy chicks? She burst out laughing. She laughed so hard she had to hold her side, tears ran down her face, and she nearly wet her pants. Whenever she'd start to wind down, he'd say *fuzzy* or *cuddly* and she'd start back up roaring with laughter. When she couldn't take one more chuckle, she called uncle.

Nolan grinned. "Changed the subject, didn't I."

"That's not exactly what I had in mind, but yes. Yes, you did. And I have now had my core training for a week."

"You're welcome. Now eat your dinner. We have a dresser to put together."

"My stomach hurts too much to eat, I think."

"These vegetables are delicious. I've never had anything like them," he said taking another huge helping from the dish.

"Oh, it's the town's secret recipe. You'll be eating them from now on. At everyone's house, at potlucks. Everywhere. You'll probably get sick and tired of them soon. Or maybe not—I still love them, so maybe you will too."

"A definite possibility. So, is that necklace you're

wearing one of your own creations? I've never seen anything like it before."

"Yes. As a matter of fact, it is. I actually made it several years ago. But it's got such expensive stones, so much gold, and it took so much time to create I'd have to charge several thousand dollars for it. And it's just never sold. I have it online but no takers, so every once in a while, I get it out and wear it. Then I polish it back up and put it away for safe keeping."

"Seems a shame to lock it away—it's very beautiful. Does it open? Yes. Wow—and even stones on the inside. Very unique."

"Sapphires inside and moonstones outside," she said.

"I like it a lot. I'd be interested in watching you work someday, if it wouldn't bother you. I like watching others work on their creations. I assume you have a web site or something on Etsy?"

"Yes, both. And my work is in galleries in Chelan and Wenatchee and a few other places. Barbara has some of my things in a small display case in the wedding area of her boutique."

They continued to eat and chat about many things until they were completely stuffed. Nolan put his fork down. "I can't eat another bite."

"That's very sad, because I have blueberry pie I was going to warm up and put ice cream on."

"Oh, well, then. Let's go put your dresser together and burn off some of this delicious dinner. We can have some pie in a while." Nolan got up, carried his plate and the empty vegetable baking dish to the sink, and started rinsing them.

"What are you doing? You're a guest and you don't need to clean."

"Don't be silly. I'm not cleaning—just rinsing my plate to put in the dishwasher."

She crossed her arms. "And the vegetable dish."

"Oh, no. The vegetable dish. Now I've done it. Completely over the top with rinsing the vegetable dish. But since I ate nearly all the vegetables and came close to licking the dish, I figure I can rinse it too." He plopped both dishes into the dishwasher, grabbed hers, rinsed it, and put it in too. "There. All done cleaning. Now, let's build stuff."

Kristen had opened the box earlier and had everything laid out for assembly. She picked up the instruction book and opened to the first page. "Step one."

Nolan took the instruction book and flung it toward the kitchen. "We don't need instructions. It's very obvious how this goes together."

"Okaaay."

A half hour later, Nolan finally relented. "Fine. Get the darn instructions. Some idiot designed this. So, we better follow the directions."

Another half hour later, after following the directions, she had a very nice dresser put together. She never said a single word and she didn't smirk. She was very proud of her restraint.

"Let's carry it into your room."

"Oh, um, no need, I'll get it in there tomorrow."

"Don't be silly. Let's get it where it belongs. Lift up your end."

So, they carried the dresser into the bedroom and after he set it down, he turned and stared—his eyes wide and his mouth hanging open. "You really did try on everything. I thought you were just making me feel better."

"Nope, really did."

He grabbed her by the waist and swung her around like she weighed nothing and was twelve. "That is so awesome. I'm so glad you were as much of a basket case as I was."

"Yeah, it's great we are both slightly insane."

"Want me to help you put it all back?"

"Uh no, I don't. Let's go eat pie." She pushed him out of her space and closed the door.

While she heated up the dessert, he cleaned up the dresser packaging and bagged it up neatly for recycling.

When she came out with blueberry pie a la mode and coffee she looked at the area and then at him. "This is getting scary."

"What?"

"Too perfect. You must have a flaw or two. No one is perfect. Or is this all pretend and you're really an axe murderer?"

"Oh, I have plenty of flaws—don't you worry about that," he said with a smile that didn't reach his eyes. A shadow crossed his face and then the moment was gone. He brightened and reached for his plate. "And being a pie pig is one of them."

She wondered what he'd been thinking, but put it aside. "Since I have a whole pie and I certainly don't need to eat all of it—pig away."

"Your wish is my command."

They sat side-by-side on the couch—eating dessert and drinking coffee—chatting about unimportant things. Farley came over and curled up by her feet.

When it was time to leave, Nolan walked to the door and she followed. He turned and asked, "So do I get a goodbye kiss too?"

"I suppose."

"Good." Nolan swooped in, pulled her close, and laid his lips on hers—kissing her like a man that had been starving and she was a five-course meal. Her heart was knocking against her ribs so hard she was sure he could feel it. She put her arms around his neck and held tight. When he pulled back she was breathless.

"Thanks for the steak. I'll have to tell Hank his cows are very tasty."

"Thank you for putting my dresser together. If I had tried to put it together I think it would have taken so much time, I'd have lost all my customers and then I'd be jobless."

Nolan laughed. "It's been a pleasure hanging out with you. Please call me anytime you need to have furniture put together. I'd be happy to help."

"I will."

Chapter Six

KRISTEN WAS WORKING away in her studio on a new piece for Vangie, with one of the cabs she'd bought at auction. She and Vangie had sent emails back and forth while they tried to design the perfect piece. They had run the risk of overflowing the small amount of storage she had on her account. So, she'd deleted some old emails from friends, with a silent apology, to make room for more iterations of the design. They had finally hit on the perfect plan. And she had decided a phone upgrade was in order—it was a vital link to her customers across the country. Not a good place to skimp.

It was hard for her to splurge on the latest and greatest—they'd been so poor growing up that she had to fight her natural instinct to get the bare-bones-only. She thought Barbara was the same way. She'd run her wedding dress business out of their home den and had done everything herself, until Chris had gotten hurt in a fire. That had opened Barbara's eyes and she'd leased the shop next door and brought on seamstresses—some of which had become her partners. She had set up their den as a hospital room and had spent all her time helping Chris recover.

Kristen wasn't sure how much the fire and Chris's injury had contributed to saving their marriage, but it seemed to be a turning point—at least in Kristen's opinion. She was happy her sister and Chris seemed to be doing really well now. Of course, getting that scheming bitch, Irene, out of town had certainly been a good move. She'd been shocked at the deviousness the woman had gone through to try to break up their marriage. Thank God Mary Ann had been living next door to the house Irene was renting and could tell Barbara the truth.

Mary Ann was in the studio with her today. She was instructing her on some new techniques for soldering. She was starting to do a few simple pieces that would help Kristen and maybe even allow Mary Ann to move into doing some of her own designs—down the road—once she learned enough. In Kristen's opinion, the world could always use more jewelry designers.

She had Mary Ann practicing the new techniques while she worked on the piece for Vangie when there was a knock on the door. Her heart leaped wondering if it could be Nolan, but when she answered it she saw it was

Gus—the town's newspaper owner and recently revealed millionaire.

"Hello, Gus." She stepped back to allow him to come in.

"Kristen, how ya doing? So, I've been hearing about your new studio. Looks mighty nice."

"Um, thanks, Gus. I like it." Kristen wondered why he was there. Gus never seemed to do much of anything without a purpose.

"So, I hear there's a nice gallery space on the first floor of the house too."

Oh no, what had he heard? "Um, yes, there is a nice area, but…."

"So, are you going ta be helping the town by opening a gallery ta show off all the goods we make here?" Gus asked with his quiet, laid back, low key, firm authority.

Aha! He was there to guilt her into opening a gallery and she really had no idea how to say no and he knew it. The beast.

"Um, I don't really have the personality to run a gallery. I need a whole lot more solitude than that and I plan to head back up the mountain as soon as it's safe."

"But ya could open it and let someone else run it. You've got the space and a good amount of your own things to put in. Seems to me Mary Ann here, could work on charms and the like, while she manned the gallery and waited for folks to show up." Looking at Mary Ann he asked, "Would ya like that?"

"Oh, yes, but it's Kristen's house and she still needs

to be happy and comfortable with the idea and not feel railroaded into it, Gus."

"Oh, not railroading. Just asking some questions and maybe hinting a bit."

Kristen felt like stomping her feet like a child, but refrained. "I'll give it some serious consideration."

"Good enough. I'm going ta mosey along. Good day ta ya ladies."

Kristen waited until she saw Gus was far enough away before she exploded. "Damn it. I don't want a gallery. But every person I've talked to thinks it would be awesome. Fine. You, Mary Ann, can open the gallery. I don't want to have anything—at all—to do with it, besides stocking it with my work. You set it up. You figure it out. You deal with it start to finish. I provide the space and my work."

"Yay! You won't regret it. I promise."

"No, I'm sure I *will* regret it, but I don't want someone coming by my studio every day asking about a gallery, so just do it."

"Okay," she said and sat there looking at Kristen with a frown.

"Spill it." Kristen folded her arms across her chest.

"I do have a few questions about it. For instance, is there some kind of contract for taking things on consignment? Do we make the sale and pay all the taxes and then pay the artists? Or do they pay the taxes and we are just the medium for the sale? Questions like that."

"Oh, you don't need to be worried about that, I have my things in galleries, so I have a contract we can use. I had a lawyer draw me up one, since he had all the knowledge about that kind of thing and I've used it with every gallery I work with. I have a pretty good handle on all those kinds of issues. And I have an accountant that keeps my finances straight so we can tap him for that. Some of the more abstract things is what I worry about. Like do we need to advertise? Do we have to have a web presence? Can we just let the town put us in the brochure and website they are creating or will we have to take the time to figure all that out? What should we name it? Will we need to hire more people or just open it a few hours each day? What if you get sick?"

Mary Ann laughed. "Okay, so it's not quite as simple as gathering a few items and unlocking the door, but it can't be too hard. Are any of the galleries you work with on friendly enough terms to ask?"

"You know, Nolan Thompson's mother has a gallery for her art, so he might have some ideas or knowledge."

"Really? What kind of art?"

"Glass. Lucille Thompson." Kristen waited to see if Mary Ann knew who she was talking about. It didn't take long for recognition to dawn.

"Are you kidding? Lucille Thompson is Nolan's mother? I love her stuff. Naturally she had to be my favorite, since we have the same last name."

Kristen shook her head. "Not kidding and he even has his own glass sculpting equipment in storage. He says he knows the mechanics but isn't creative, but I'm not sure I believe it."

"Wow. That's amazing. Maybe we could get a few of her pieces, too. Wouldn't that be awesome?"

Kristen nodded. That idea was the only redeeming factor in this whole plan, as far as she was concerned. "I'll get in touch with him and see what he has to say."

"That would be so cool. I'm wondering if I should keep practicing what you taught me this morning or sit down and make some lists and plans. It will be an eclectic assortment of artists and art."

"Yeah, not your normal gallery for certain." Kristen chuckled.

"Normal is overrated and usually a bunch of lies anyway. I think it will be fun. So, you're getting pretty chummy with the new police officer."

Kristen shook her head. "Just friends. Any word from the hotshots on the fire?"

"Not much. Trey came into town the other day. One of the guys had gotten hurt and needed to be seen by the doctor. He'd lost some blood and was kind of pale by the time they got him here. But the doc fixed him up."

"Trey, huh. Are you getting chummy with Trey?"

"Boy, I'd love that. He is a hunk." Mary Ann grinned. "We had some laughs at Greg's bar while he was in town, but then he went back up and I didn't even get a kiss. What's wrong with these guys? They can't even spare a little lip-lock."

"Um, I have no idea." Kristen looked around guiltily, trying to find something to say.

Mary Ann was no fool. "Kristen, have you been making out with the new cop in town?"

"I have nothing to say."

Mary Ann laughed. "You have! And you've been holding out. Let's hear the deets."

Kristen shrugged and felt her face heat. "Just a kiss or two. No big deal, really."

"Then why are you seven shades of red?"

"I repeat: I have nothing to say."

"Well, let me just say, you go girl!"

"Mary Ann, you are incorrigible." Kristen folded her arms.

"And not nearly as lucky as you, so I'll have to live vicariously."

"Or grab Trey the next time he's in town and lay a big fat one on him."

Mary Ann shook her head. "Oh, I couldn't do that."

"Why not, it works like a charm."

"What? Are you telling me *you* grabbed Officer Thompson and kissed *him?*"

"Maybe."

"Whoo hoo. You are totally my hero!" Mary Ann clapped her hands and then put them on her hips. "And here you are pretending to be this shy little recluse."

"Not shy—just not a *bunch-of-people-at-a-time* person and I have to work alone to get the creative juices flowing."

"I think I need to tap into your mysterious charisma, encourage the hottie firefighter to give me a little smooch."

"You go right ahead." Kristen shrugged. "But it's really

just grabbing him and kissing him. Most men don't need too much encouragement. Just a nice solid hint, or in this case, a kiss."

"I bow to your expertise and wisdom."

"Okay, play time is over. Back to work."

"Yes, ma'am."

As Kristen worked, she thought about having a gallery and more importantly about having Nolan come back to ask him about setting one up. That might be the only perk to allowing everyone to railroad her into a gallery. She should also talk to her sister and Chris, since he'd done most of the paperwork to get Barbara's boutique up. Kristen laughed to herself thinking her and Barbara had both been railroaded into a show room. She could just imagine the look on Barbara's face when she walked into that house thinking she'd find a sewing area and had walked into a very nice boutique. There was a sewing area, of course—just on the second floor. Barbara had been too softhearted to make them dismantle the store front and she'd been too busy helping Chris with his injury to deal with it. What had started out as a short-term lease had turned into a very profitable partnership with the other ladies. Not so funny, now that the shoe was on the other foot, so to speak. Oh, well. She could always go back up the mountain and leave Mary Ann to deal with it. Yeah, sure she could. She wasn't controlling. She wasn't a perfectionist. She wasn't a firstborn. Nope she could let it go, easy-peasy. Just not in this lifetime.

So, she sent Nolan a text.

Would like to pick your son-of-Lucille brain. Have pie left over.

Interesting. I'll bring pizza. Off at six.

Perfect.

Chapter Seven

NOLAN ORDERED A PIZZA FOR six-thirty and went home to change. He had no idea what *son-of-Lucille brain* meant but he wasn't turning down the offer to spend more time with the foxy lady. When he got to her house every light was on in the downstairs gallery area, so he went to that door and knocked. She opened it quickly and yanked him inside.

"What's going on?"

"I'm weak and giving in."

"You are in no way weak. What are you giving in to?"

"A gallery in this space." Kristen whined.

"Oh. Well, it would be an awesome one."

"Yes, I know. But I know nothing—less than nothing, super negative nothing—about opening or running a gallery. I certainly have some of my work in other people's galleries, but I know nothing, less than—"

Nolan's eyes widened. "Okay, yeah, got it. Let's go upstairs, eat pizza, and talk. Then we can come down and look around. Is that cool? We don't want to eat cold pizza, after all."

"Good idea." She grabbed his hand and started dragging him to the stairs.

Nolan dug in his heels and yanked her back to him. He put their joined hands around behind her, against her back, and pulled her up tight against his body. Holding the pizza above them he lowered his head and kissed her long and hard.

When he finally felt her relax against him, he lifted his head and said, "Now, breathe. We got this."

She took a deep breath and sighed. "Okay."

When they got upstairs, he put the pizza on the table, pushed her into a chair, and got them both a beer and hunted around for plates.

He gave her the beer. "Drink."

He put two slices of pizza on a plate and slid it in front of her. "Eat."

"But—"

"No talking. Eat. Drink. That's all… Unless you want to go back to kissing. I think that would be acceptable too. Or having sex—yeah, that would work."

She laughed and took a big bite of pizza.

"Damn," he muttered.

They ate in silence.

WHEN SHE PUSHED her plate away and drained her beer, he asked, "More pizza? Another beer?"

"No, I'm full, but thanks. I was freaking out a little."

"You're an artist. It's what you do, when confronted with an unplanned obstacle that isn't in your field of comfort."

"So says the Little Guy."

He laughed. "Yep. Been there a few times. So as long as it's not going to cue the freaking out, want to tell me about it?"

"I think I'm done freaking for now. It's just, everyone that's seen the house has commented on how great a gallery set up it is. Then today Gus came by to give me a backhanded push to do it. He even asked Mary Ann if she'd run it. I just have to provide the space and yada yada yada."

"Gus? The newspaper man? How does he have any authority...."

"Ah, yes. The new kid in town has bought into the laid back, country bumpkin, illusion." Kristen nodded.

"Oh? Tell me more."

"The man has millions—maybe billions—and has helped a lot of people in town over hurdles to keep them going. He doesn't hand it out, he invests in people working to make it. He bought Amber a new stove. Basically, fully funded the Amusement Park—well, half of it anyway. The game company ponied up for a number of rides too. But Gus got the ball rolling with fifty million."

Nolan whistled. "Seriously? The guy steals sugar and jelly from Amber's and makes everyone else pay for his meals."

She patted his arm. "So, you're *not* just a pretty face. You've noticed his antics."

He pointed to his chest. "Uh, cop. It's what we do."

"Anyway, he came in, to put some pressure on me. So now I need to open the gallery and as much as I'd like to hand it over to Mary Ann, I'm much too big of a control freak to do that. So, I know I will be knee-deep, so to speak, and called to see if you had any pointers."

"Ah. That explains the *son-of-Lucille* reference. Okay, then. Let's go look at your space."

She folded her arms across her chest. "Don't wanna."

"Come on now. It's what I'm here for."

"Can we have sex instead?"

Nolan's eyes turned hot, but then he shook his head. "As much as it pains me to say this. No. Downstairs. Now."

Kristen pouted. "Fine, but I'm not offering again."

"Now, that's just mean."

"Yes, it is, but not as mean as you making me go downstairs."

"We could take another beer with us." Nolan smiled.

"I think tequila would be better."

He laughed and yanked her out of her chair. "Come on, control freak. Let's do this."

They went downstairs and Kristen told him about some of the suggestions Mary Ann had come up with.

He looked carefully at each location and the lighting. "Yes, I could see that. My mother's glass would look good right here where there is a lot of light and not much behind it. Glass is better with a wall or something solid behind it so things don't reflect. But it also needs a lot of light so it shines. You can see this corner from the door too and since it's toward the back people will have to walk through the rest of the main room to get to it."

"Oh, do you think she'd let us put some in our gallery?"

"I think I could convince her."

"Yeah? Yay. That would be amazing." She grabbed him around the neck and put little kisses all over his face saying, "I love it," after each kiss.

"That's some enthusiasm I could get behind."

Kristen laughed and then they heard a crash outside. Farley came racing down the stairs barking like crazy. Nolan pulled the gun from his ankle and suddenly was all cop—the teasing, laughing man was gone. "Stay here and lock the door behind me."

He went out the door and shut it behind him. Farley whined to go with him, so she grabbed his collar. Kristen didn't lock the door. Instead, she looked out to see what the noise could have been. It looked like her trash cans were knocked over. That was something she dealt with on a regular basis. On her mountain, between the bears and the raccoon armies that often invaded her trash, this was normal stuff. Nolan walked around the house and apparently decided the same thing, so he came back to the door. When she saw him coming back, she let Farley out to sniff around.

She was still standing there with the door open, so he frowned at her. "What part of *lock the door behind me* did you not understand?"

"You do realize I live alone, on the top of the mountain, and don't normally have a big bad cop at my beck and call—so I have to face the wildlife alone."

"Yes, I realize that, but it doesn't necessarily mean I like the idea. And you aren't in the wilderness here—it could have been something or someone besides wildlife."

"Did you see anyone or anything else?" she asked.

"No, but I didn't see any wildlife either, so I don't know what it was."

Farley came back to the door, having sniffed around and done his dog thing. Kristen watched him walk into the house. "It looks like trash cans knocked over, which would be a good indication it was wildlife sniffing around for a snack, like bears or a raccoon army."

"A raccoon army?"

She smiled. "Well, that's what I call the little beggars when they are scattering trash all over the yard."

"I see. It's entirely possible that's what knocked over the trash cans, but it also could have been a clumsy person."

"I don't like that idea, so I choose wildlife." She nodded her head sharply.

"Fine. And I think that's my cue to head home. I'll talk to my mom about sending some of her pieces. I was thinking it might be time for her to send my glass making paraphernalia too."

"Oh, I'd love to see it all and how it works. Do you want to take the rest of the pizza home?"

Nolan shook his head. "No, you keep it. I know you artists, you'll get busy with something and forget to eat. So, you can save it for emergency food, since pizza is good cold or hot."

"Yeah, I could get behind that. Thanks for coming over. As we get this going, would you mind if I pestered you with questions?"

"I'd not mind at all. In fact, I look forward to it— especially if we can end the night with a small goodbye kiss. Or maybe a big one." He took her hand and she walked right into him, went up on her toes, and lifted her face toward him. That seemed to be enough invitation and he kissed her. He started with brushing his lips back and forth. His tongue touched her mouth and she parted for him. The kiss got deeper and he tasted like pizza and beer and a special taste that was all Nolan. Yum. Quite the combination. They kissed until they ran out of air and their hearts were pounding in tandem. She dropped down from her toes and laid her head on his chest to listen as his heart beat for her. It was a delightful sound.

Nolan laid his chin on the top of her head. "Bubbles."

"Bubbles?"

"Yes, it feels like thousands of bubbles floating and bursting inside me when I kiss you. Like Champaign. Amazing."

"Hmm. Well, that's a unique way to describe it, but you may be right. Bubbles indeed."

"Good night, Kristen. Have a good sleep."

"Good night, Nolan. I'll be calling you soon."

"Anytime you want. I'll let you know what my mother says and if she has any pointers."

She did lock the door after him, this time. And she and Farley went up to bed. Glass art and champagne bottles artfully arranged in the gallery filled her dreams—along with bubbles, hot kisses, and a lot of nakedness.

Chapter Eight

KRISTEN DIDN'T HEAR FROM Nolan for three days and she decided it was his turn to initiate contact. Just when she had decided he wasn't going to call, he appeared at her workshop door—with his mother. His mother? Here in Chedwick after only three days? How was that even possible? An airline flight and a shuttle took longer than that. She would have had to blast out the door the minute she talked to Nolan to arrive this quickly.

"Kristen, this is my mom, Lucille. Mom, this is Kristen. She's the jewelry artist who's going to be opening a gallery soon."

"Yes, I figured that, in fact, that's why I'm here—to meet this woman who has you thinking about art again." Lucille barged into Kristen's studio with a waft of expensive perfume. "Nice to meet you, Kristen. This studio must be a joy to work in. So bright and open, lots of space to spread out and still not look cluttered."

Kristen stepped back to make room. "It is. I can't take credit for it though. The previous owners were painters and they set it all up. It was the major selling point, however."

"Certainly, it would be. Any real artist would love the space. Let's see the gallery. Nolan said it's on the first floor of the house. You have living quarters upstairs?"

"Yes, I'd be happy to show you around." Not that she had any choice. Nolan's mother was a force to be reckoned with.

Lucille said, "Nolan says you are planning on quite a mish-mash of art. It's not always wise to mix so many mediums."

"It's really going to be a place to showcase the artisans in town, more than a traditional gallery."

"Interesting."

Nolan rolled his eyes at his mother's highhandedness and Kristen tried not to laugh when they went across the yard to the house.

As they walked through the space, Nolan pointed out the plans Kristen had told him about. When they got to the area he'd suggested for his mother, he didn't point it out. Kristen thought that odd, but just waited to see what would happen.

"Oh, and this is where my art would go. It is perfect for it, with just the right lighting and correct angles to showcase my work. Perfect—and I know just which pieces to send. Excellent. I'll stay here for a while and talk art and contracts with Kristen. You go on back to work now, son, and we can all go out to eat after you're through working."

Nolan looked from his mother to Kristen. "But—"

"No buts, you have to finish out your day—even if it is just a couple of hours. Run along now, Kristen and I will be fine."

Nolan looked at Kristen who shrugged.

When he had driven off, Kristen looked at Lucille. "Shall we go upstairs for some tea?"

"Yes and if you can put a shot of whiskey in it that would make it even better. I've had a long three days trying to get here this quickly."

"I did wonder how you managed that. I have a nice bottle of Tennessee Honey which is great in tea—or coffee if you prefer. Another great mixture is vanilla coke and whiskey."

"Sold!"

Kristen made drinks for both of them. She decided a little false courage might be a good thing. "So why did you come here so quickly?"

Taking a large drink Lucille smiled her pleasure. "Oh, I said it before. I had to meet the woman who got my son thinking about his art again."

"He said he can do it, but he's not creative." Kristen took a drink and felt the whiskey warm her, while the taste was like butterscotch candy.

"He rejected his talent. Once he decided on the police force, he wouldn't even discuss it. Did he tell you why he joined the police?"

"No. In fact, I've gotten very little personal information from him. He always turns the conversation back to me or gets me laughing."

"Not a surprise to his mother. I'll tell you the story and then you'll understand a lot more about him." She took another big drink. "I'm going to need this to get through the telling, but if you have him thinking about art, you have done something none of the rest of us have been able to do. So, you must be special to him and will need to know this."

"We're just friends," Kristen said, although she could feel her face heat as she said that.

"Right. He was a senior in high school and he was working on a big project that he was going to put into a competition." She sighed. "His twin sister tracked him down in the art room. She wanted to go to the football game and wanted him to come with her. He brushed her off and told her he was too busy with his art project to go to a stupid game." Lucille held on tightly to the glass. "So, she went alone. He stayed and finished his piece and put it in the kiln for completion and cool down; his teacher would box it up two days later and take it to the competition.

"Nolan came home after that to sleep—he'd been putting in a lot of hours to get his piece perfect. The next morning, we asked him where his sister was. He said she'd gone to the game, so we called around to her friends to see if she'd gone home with one of them. They said she'd never shown up at the game and they had assumed she'd changed her mind. The police found her body a week later in a field outside of town. She'd been kidnapped, repeatedly raped, and then strangled in some kind of ritual killing." A single tear ran down her face, she wiped it away and cleared her throat.

"Nolan blamed himself for not going with her. When he won first place in the competition he turned down the offer of ten thousand dollars for the piece. Then he took the sculpture, the blue ribbon, the first-place certificate, and the five hundred dollars' prize money to the field his sister had been found in. He burned the ribbon, certificate, and money and then beat the sculpture into shards. He never worked on glass again and he joined the police academy after graduation. We put his equipment into storage, hoping that someday he'd learn to forgive himself and use it again."

Kristen had tears running down her face by the end of the story. Both Kristen and Lucille took a long drink, she needed it to get the lump in her throat to go down.

"That's the saddest thing I have ever heard. Now I see why you got here so quickly."

"Nothing on earth could have stopped me. So how did you meet my son?"

Kristen related the story to Lucille who sat there with her mouth hanging open. "You stayed on that mountain, with fire all around you, and waited for some guys to show up to help you move those tanks? That's extremely brave of you."

"At the time, I was terrified—but determined someone would show up in time, so that those tanks didn't blow up and kill everything on the top of the mountain. When Nolan first arrived all he could see was that I wasn't following the directions. But once I dragged him and the fire jumper or hotshot actually; I hear there is a difference. Anyway, once I dragged them both into the shed, Nolan changed his tune with a quickness."

Lucille laughed. "I never said he was a stupid man, and I have acetylene tanks for my art, so it didn't take him two looks to know what they were."

"I can tell you I was never so glad to see a big, strong man in my life when I turned around and saw him standing there frowning at me."

"So, how can I help you with the gallery?"

"I know nothing about a gallery or running one and, quite frankly, I never wanted to know. I'm a bit of a recluse."

"No. Really? Living at the top of a mountain on what is little more than a glorified goat trail, with only your dog for company. Recluse? Just a touch." Lucille's eyes sparkled with mirth.

"Anyway, nearly everyone who saw the space downstairs tried to talk me into opening a gallery. But it was Gus, the newspaper multi-millionaire, that finally guilted me into it. And I really thought I could just let my helper—Mary Ann—do it all, but I'm much too much of a control freak to let it go. So here I am. What can you tell me?"

"How about I stick around for a while, harass my son, and help you get it going. I can call my assistant and she can ship the pieces I have in mind to put in here."

"You really want to put some of your art in my

fledgling, mixed up gallery?"

"Yes. And if I help you, I have the perfect excuse to hang around a while longer and see if Nolan is really going to use that equipment I'm having shipped here. It should be here by next week, so we'll see what happens then."

Kristen felt her throat catch again as she thought of all he'd been through and decided, in comparison, her life had been a piece of cake.

"So, would you mind terribly if I relax for an hour? Maybe on your couch? I'm a little worn out from my mad dash here."

"I actually just got a bed in the spare room, so let me show you to it and you can take a nap. Nolan usually gets off work about six and is here by six-thirty."

"Oh. *Usually*, huh. Very interesting."

"Just as friends, of course." Kristen felt her face heat and turned to lead Lucille to the guest room.

NOLAN HAD BEEN surprised when his mother had called him from the ferry to come pick her up. He'd phoned her when he'd gotten home from Kristen's knowing her work hours went late into the night, so late chats were fine. But call early in the morning, and a person was on the top of her shit list for days or weeks, even. His phone conversation had ended up with unexpected results, since she'd dropped everything and been to town within three days. Hell, it had taken him a week to make the same trip and that was after the airline tickets were booked. He wasn't quite sure how she'd pulled it off, but the woman had skills he'd never been able to figure out. Was it normal to think your mother was some kind of wizard or miracle worker?

His shift was over in a half hour and then he'd head home to change clothes before taking his ladies out for dinner. *His* ladies? Was he really thinking of Kristen that way? Obviously, he was. Did he like that he was thinking of her that way? Maybe he did. He hoped they were getting along okay—his mother was a strong-willed woman and so was Kristen. He supposed they would become friends or kill each other. He was rooting for the former.

He called Amber's and asked if he needed to make reservations for the fine dining side of the restaurant. They took his booking. He went home, put his mother's suitcase in his guest room, and changed clothes. He knocked on Kristen's back door at six thirty. He heard his mother laugh and Kristen answered the door with a slight blush. He wondered what his mother and Kristen had been talking about.

"I got us reservations for seven thirty."

Lucille asked, "Is my suitcase here? I'd like to change clothes."

"Oh man, I didn't even think about you wanting to change. I left your suitcase at home."

Kristen laughed. "I'm sure I have something that would fit. We aren't too different in size. Let's see if we can find something. And I need to change too, if we are going to eat in the reservations side of the restaurant."

"Okay, but make it snappy ladies. We don't have all night."

At seven fifteen Nolan hollered, "We're running out of time."

"We're coming."

Nolan looked up from the newspaper he was reading and whistled. "You both look lovely. So, it was worth the wait." His mother had on a pretty blue dress with polka dots and Kristen had on a peach colored sundress and strappy sandals. He got up and kissed them both on the cheek. "I'm going to be the most envied man in the restaurant tonight."

"Laying it on pretty thick, Little Guy," Kristen drawled.

Nolan rolled his eyes and groaned dramatically.

Lucille laughed. "You are my kind of woman Kristen—and perfect for keeping my son in his place. Let's go, Little Guy."

"Six foot four, over two hundred pounds and I'm still Little Guy," he muttered. "I could bench press them. Maybe both of them at the same time. Little Guy my ass."

Kristen and Lucille laughed out loud as he mumbled all the way to the car.

Chapter Nine

KRISTEN STARTED HEARING FROM the different artists in the area. The word had gotten out that she was opening the gallery and everyone seemed to be very excited. When they had walked into Amber's the other night and Amber had mentioned Kristen opening a place for artists to display and sell their work, Kristen knew that the word had spread—despite owning the primary restaurant in town, Amber was always the last to know anything. She didn't like gossip and everyone knew it, so they didn't share.

Since even Amber knew about the gallery, Kristen called up Mary Ann and asked her to plan to stick around her place for the next few days. Her cell phone was ringing off the hook with people asking about the plans, she needed to get a business number immediately. Some of the artists planned to start bringing their art by to stock it. She was telling each artist to contact her lawyer to fill out the contracts, *then* they could bring their art by. She wanted Mary Ann to handle as much as she could, so Kristen could keep working on the pieces she had on order.

Lucille was a surprise gift; she was also spending a lot of time at the gallery to help get things set up. With Mary Ann and Lucille taking the deliveries and arranging things, Kristen felt safe to continue on with her projects. In the back of her mind she thought about what pieces of her own she'd like to display. Certainly, the one she'd created a number of years ago and never sold due to the cost. She had a few things she made in bulk and a few she had made up for stock. She had a lot of custom commission pieces right now so she didn't have a lot of time to make new things.

When Kristen was done for the day she took some jewelry out of her safe, closed up the studio, and went over to look at the progress. "Doesn't this look awesome? You guys did a great job. It looks very professional but also cozy—so many galleries have such a stiff, formal feel, I sometimes feel nervous wandering through them, but you've hit just the right note of comfort.

"Here are some things of mine to add to the collection. I'll try to get a few more things ready. I noticed there were some unfinished projects in the safe that I had started for people and then the commission fell through, so those won't take a lot of time to get completed. Especially if Mary Ann can help with the polishing."

"I'd be happy to."

Lucille asked, "So could you teach me to help? I think it would be fun to work in a different medium for a while even if it's just the cleanup. It never hurts to try new things."

Kristen shook her head. "I can't imagine someone as talented as you are and so renown, would want to do cleanup."

"I think it would be fun."

"Fine with me. I can show you—or Mary Ann can. We have some charms Mary Ann works on." She looked at Mary Ann, "Maybe we should set up a small work area over here, so that while you keep an eye on the gallery, you can also be working on the charms when it's slow."

Marry Ann nodded. "There is that area off to the side that might be perfect for that. It has good natural light and a view of the showroom."

"Okay, let's do that. We need to get the buffer over here from your house and we could set up a little workstation. We'd need to set up a plastic enclosure, to keep the buffing medium from getting all over everything. But that shouldn't be too hard."

Lucille spoke up, "I'm sure we could get Nolan to help move whatever needs to be brought over. He is freakishly strong."

"That would be great, whenever he has the time. I imagine you'll be kept busy for a few more days as people continue to drop things off for display. But right now, I need to take my poor dog for a walk, I've been neglecting him lately. He can't run free in town like he does on the mountain."

"Oh? Where do you take him?" Lucille asked.

"Today, I think we'll go down by the lake, he likes to be by the water."

Lucille brightened. "Would you mind if I come along? I haven't seen much of the lake."

"Sure, come along."

Mary Ann said, "If we're done for the day I'm going to head out. I *might* have a hot date with a hotshot. He called and said he might have the weekend off. A new crew came in yesterday."

"Remember what we talked about, and I'll see you Monday."

Mary Ann laughed. "I just might follow your advice."

Kristen got Farley's leash. He saw her get it and started turning circles in his enthusiasm for a walk. "Okay, enough. Sit, Farley."

He sat mid spin and quivered with happiness as Kristen put him on the leash. When they got to the lake, they walked through the sand along the shore while Farley ran in and out of the water.

Lucille laughed. "Someone is going to see those zigzagging footprints in the sand and wonder what was going on."

Kristen felt her phone vibrate in her pocket. She saw Lucille reach for hers at the same time. Nolan had sent them both a text asking if they wanted to grill at his house for dinner. They looked at each other, nodded and sent him a text agreeing to the idea.

Kristen said, "Let's go by Samantha's bakery on the way back and pick up something for dessert."

"I like the way you think, Kristen."

By the time, they finally got Farley to stop playing in the water, stopped by the bakery, and walked back to the gallery, it was time to head over to Nolan's.

Lucille walked in the door. "How was your day today, my son?"

"Good. We had a high-speed chase."

Kristen gasped. "A high-speed chase? In Chedwick? Really?"

"Yep. We had to chase down a hardened criminal after a theft."

Kristen and Lucille both looked at him waiting for more details. The warmth Kristen had felt when she walked in and saw him evaporated into a cold knot of fear that he'd been in danger

He finally caved. "I ran down the street to stop a kid on his bicycle after he stole a candy bar from the store."

Kristen and Lucille both laughed with relief and Nolan said, "Gotcha."

Lucille crossed her arms. "Humph, just for that we may not let you have any pie."

"Pie? You brought pie?"

Kristen put her hands on her hips. "Yes, and you can't have any for scaring us."

"That's mean." Nolan pouted.

"What is that sound I hear?" Lucille said, "Oh, yes. It's the sound of paybacks."

"All I did was pull your leg a little and you are going to deprive me of pie? How is that fair? What kind of pie?"

"Blackberry."

"Hey, that's my favorite!"

Lucille smirked. "Which is why we bought it."

"So, you *are* going to let me have some—you wouldn't want to see a grown man cry, now would you?"

Kristen shrugged. "Oh, I suppose not; it wouldn't be a very pretty sight. Yes, you can have some pie as long as you do a good job feeding us beforehand. What are we having?"

"Spare ribs, potato salad, watermelon, and corn-on-the-cob." Nolan puffed out his chest.

Kristen and Lucille looked at each other and nodded.

Kristen said, "Okay, you win the pie."

"Yay. Let's get cookin'!"

Kristen chopped up the watermelon, while Lucille made the potato salad. Nolan manned the grill. Like any alpha male on the planet, the grill was his domain. Lucille sent Kristen out with the corn wrapped in foil, butter and seasoning sealed inside. The smell of meat filled the air and there was a pleasant breeze blowing—just enough to cool her off after working in the kitchen.

Nolan moved the cooked ribs to the side to keep warm and he put the corn on the grill. Then—before she knew what he had in mind—he whisked her off to the side of the patio out of view of the kitchen, pushed her up against the wall, and kissed her. Long and hard and hungry. She felt his urgency and gave it right back to him.

When he lifted his head, he panted. "Wow, I needed that. It's seems like forever since I last kissed you."

"I'm sure it's been weeks and weeks."

Lucille said, "I have been here five days."

Startled, Kristen and Nolan jumped apart.

Lucille continued, "And no one said you couldn't kiss the girl because I'm here."

"Mom," Nolan whined, "no one wants their mother to see them kissing."

"Afraid I'll critique you?"

Kristen laughed.

Nolan cringed, then shrugged and straightened his shoulders, "If you did, I'd get high scores."

"Uh huh. I think you're burning the corn."

Chapter Ten

NOLAN HADN'T BURNED THE CORN, but it was a bit singed. The dinner was delicious and as they ate Kristen and his mother told him all about the progress on the gallery. He was happy to hear all the details and thought it all sounded like it was coming together very well. Part of his brain was focused on that kiss earlier. He really felt like he'd been starving for her—it was a very strange feeling. Why would he be feeling that way? She was beautiful, but so were a lot of other women. She was brave, but again, so were a lot of other women. He couldn't put his finger on why she was so different from any other female he'd ever known.

"Nolan. Earth to Nolan." His mother snapped her fingers in front of his face.

Startled, he focused on her. "What?"

"I said, how about if you make us some decaf while we clear the table and then we can have pie and coffee."

"Oh, good idea. On the deck under the stars. Or in this case, since it's summer in the Pacific Northwest, under the bright blue sky." His mother and Kristen laughed at his joke and Nolan escaped to the coffee maker. He ground the beans of his special coffee, which filled the room with a pleasant aroma. He had a friend who had moved to Hawaii, on the big island, so he had a hookup for the best Kona coffee—at least in his friend's opinion. The people also grew macadamia nuts and they had a special family recipe for processing them. The nuts were crisp and perfectly seasoned. They were the best he'd ever had, but they didn't grow a lot of them so they were a treasure.

He got out the cream he always kept for his coffee and his mother's. He'd been spoiled with real cream in his coffee and he almost couldn't drink it without it. Almost— he was a cop, after all, and often didn't have any choice in the matter. But when he was home he always pampered himself with Kona brew, so he just couldn't use milk or god forbid that powdered stuff..

He put the cream into a little glass pitcher he used when he had company—especially his mother. He put that and the matching sugar bowl on a tray with cups. He poured the java into a carafe and carried it all out to the deck. The women followed with warmed pie a la mode.

They sat outside in the warm summer evening, eating their pie and watched as dusk approached. When they were finished his mother got up. "Well, I'm going to my room now to watch TV. Nolan, you really should follow Kristen home to take a look at the gallery."

"Oh that's not—" Kristen started to say.

"Now, Kristen, don't deprive him of seeing all that we have accomplished and seeing you home at the same time." His mother whispered, "So he can steal another kiss."

Kristen turned bright red and Nolan held in a chuckle. His mother, bless her heart, was matchmaking. Not that he was going to complain. Nope. In fact, he planned to do just as she suggested and if Kristen was open to it, he might just take it to the next level.

As his mother went off to her room, Nolan carried their dessert things into the kitchen. "So are you going to let me follow you home and see all the work they put in on the gallery?"

"I don't really think that's necessary."

"No it's not, but my mother insisted and I should always obey my mother."

"Using your mother against me doesn't seem very fair."

"But this is not a fair fight. People fight dirty when it comes to romance. You know—All's fair in love and war."

"Romance?"

"Romance."

"Fine, Romeo, you can follow me home and fight unfairly all you want. Maybe I'll just encourage some dirty fighting."

"Whoa." The look in her eye was hot and hungry. He had no intention of turning that down. "I'll be right back."

He made a beeline for his room and stuffed several strips of condoms in his pocket.

He raced back to the kitchen. "Let's go then. It looks like we've got some things to accomplish tonight."

They got to her house and looked around the gallery. He made the appropriate noises of approval and asked some semi-intelligent questions. But in all reality, his brain and most of his body was focused on that hot look she'd given him and where that might lead. Kristen showed him where they wanted the workroom and he agreed to help Mary Ann move her equipment into the space next week. Finally, the tour was finished.

"Um, would you like to come upstairs for coffee or something?" Kristen asked shyly.

He took her hand and brought it to his lips. He looked her in the eye and let his desire show. "I'd love to go upstairs with you, but not for coffee. Do you want to take this to the next level? If you aren't ready, that's fine with me, but I'm not going to lie. I'm fairly certain if I come upstairs with you, we are going to be getting naked. So, if you're not ready, I should probably go home."

Kristen's eyes heated. "Come upstairs with me, Nolan."

"My pleasure." He kissed her knuckles and then ran his thumb across them as they shut off the lights and locked the doors.

Kristen hoped she wasn't making the biggest mistake of her life, but she really wanted this man. She'd been thinking and dreaming about having sex with him since the first day they met. Was she ready? She was more than ready. She just didn't want things to get awkward. She liked him and his mother and she didn't want to jeopardize their friendship.

The man brought out tingles in her with every touch, every look. And when he kissed her it wasn't just tingles—it was lightning. Like standing outside in an electrical storm. Her hair stood on end, her skin pebbled, and her pulse raced. In fact, being struck by lightning might be less forceful than Nolan's kisses.

As they walked up the stairs together she felt her body ready itself for his. The anticipation was killing her, but it was so delicious she reveled in it. When they went in the door, Farley met them.

Nolan laughed at the dog. "How about I let Farley out for a minute and you can relax or whatever."

"That sounds great."

While Nolan let the dog out, Kristen checked the bedroom—she wanted to make sure nothing weird was out in either the bathroom or the bedroom. She also turned down the bed and put her shoes in the closet. When she came out of the closet Nolan was leaning against the bedroom doorframe. His form filled the space and she shivered in anticipation of all that man surrounding her and filling her.

"That was fast," she said.

Nolan smiled. "I didn't encourage him to linger."

"Good, now come inside and shut the door—so he doesn't come to see what we're doing."

"I gave him a treat to keep him occupied."

"Smart man."

"Smart enough to know you are a beautiful woman inside and out. How did I get so lucky that you want to be with me?"

"Being new to town helps. I don't know that you wet your pants in first grade or sucked your thumb or ate paste. I don't know you pushed girls down when playing dodge ball."

Nolan laughed. "Then I'll keep my bad schoolroom behavior to myself. You can pretend I grew up full of wisdom and charm."

"Good. Now, are you just going to stand there talking all night, or are you going to kiss me?"

"Kissing seems like an excellent idea."

"Still talking, Nolan."

He drew her close. "Bossy—I like that." He pressed his lips to hers, wrapped his arms around her, and hauled her up against him. His whole body was hard against her soft one. His arms wrapped her in a cocoon of warmth and strength. He smelled amazing—all man—with a hint of soap or maybe aftershave. His mouth on hers was perfect. His tongue darted out and he licked her. She gasped at the wet warmth—it was delicious. He swept inside and she gloried in the sensation. He tasted like coffee and the pie they had eaten earlier. But his own unique taste was even better than the pie. She moaned in the back of her throat and she could feel him get harder. She pressed her hips to his, enjoying the feel of his erection against her.

"Too many clothes," he whispered, and she couldn't agree more.

She ran her hands down his back and started pulling the shirt tails out of his jeans. He fumbled with the buttons on her blouse. She pulled his T-shirt off over his head and hummed with pleasure at the sight before her, then ran her hands down his chest. Warm skin and hard muscles gave her fingers pleasure while fire raced through her veins.

Nolan finally got her shirt unbuttoned and pushed it off her shoulders. He looked at her pink bra and swallowed. "Nice. Very pretty." He cupped her curves and ran his thumbs over the nipples, the abrasion of the bra only heightening the sensations.

Kristen scraped her fingernails over his chest in return and he groaned. "Still too many clothes." He reached behind her, undid her bra, and pulled it off in a swift movement. She pressed her chest against his and brushed it back and forth, loving the feeling of skin on skin. Liquid heat shot through her and he got even harder, longer. How that was possible, she didn't know—but those jeans had to be uncomfortable.

"Let's get these jeans off, before you explode them."

He laughed and undid his belt so he could put it and his weapon on the dresser. She eagerly started in on the buttons on his fly, but it was hard to get them undone and with each brush of her hand his erection jumped.

"I don't seem to be helping—maybe you should do it."

"Yeah, button flies are great…except in this case." He quickly undid the fly and grabbed the condoms out of his pocket. She smiled as she helped push the jeans down his legs. She caressed his cock through the boxers and he groaned. "Oh baby, that feels great."

"Yeah, well, we're just getting started." She pushed his shorts off and took him in her hand. Rubbing her thumb across the head, a drop of pearly liquid escaped.

He gasped. "You need to stop that or we won't get to the main event."

"We could get to the main event a little later."

"Nope. The first time, I want to be inside you, deep inside."

"Fine by me." She unzipped her jeans and kicked them off while he swept her damp panties down her legs.

He dropped to his knees and kissed her belly and trailed more kisses south. She squeaked. "Nolan."

"Yes, baby. Just having a little taste of the promised land." He licked her softly and she nearly collapsed. "Can't have you falling." He stood and carried her over to the edge of the bed and set her down. After putting the handful of condoms on the bedside table, he dropped back to his knees and put her legs over her shoulders. "Much better." Then he parted her folds and licked her again. She collapsed back onto the bed as his tongue pleasured her most sensitive places.

"Mmm, you taste so good."

The vibration caused her body to tense and he settled in on the one spot that would send her to paradise.

When he slipped in one finger and caressed her from the inside—while his tongue caressed the outside—she melted from the feeling he was giving her. When he slipped a second digit in, she felt her body gathering for release and she clutched the sheets with both hands. As the orgasm claimed her, she tensed, her back bowed, and she pressed her hips up to his mouth, so he sucked her clit—which caused the sensations to increase in strength. He gentled the pressure as she collapsed back onto the bed. She just laid there, totally boneless, breathing hard.

He pulled her legs off his shoulders and drew her up higher on the bed with him, as he climbed in beside her. Since she couldn't function, in any way, she let him do as he pleased. He pulled her up against him and held her while she came back to herself. She felt so safe in his arms.

Finally, she whispered, "That was amazing—the most amazing thing ever. Wow."

He kissed her hair and whispered, "We're just getting started, honey."

"There's more?"

"Oh, yeah. Much more—that was just the appetizer."

"Oh, my."

He slid a finger inside of her and her body clamped around it. "You like?"

"Yes. You seem to have just the right touch."

She reached down to take him in hand. He was very hard and so smooth. Silk over marble but warm—almost hot. She felt another drop of moisture slip out of the top and she rubbed her thumb in it and smoothed it over the top.

"So, could we put all this hardness to better use."

"It would be my pleasure." He reached over to the bedside table and grabbed a strip of condoms and tore one off. With his teeth. Then opened it the same way. She helped him roll it on. He wasn't sure he'd last to get inside her, with her strong hands on him.

She rolled onto her back and opened her legs and he was quick to accept her implied invitation.

As he slid inside stretching her, filling her, she sighed. "Mmm. Nice."

He groaned. "You are so tight and hot and wet. Like heaven right here on earth."

"Too much talking. Faster, Nolan."

"Yes, ma'am."

Each thrust lifted her higher and higher. She felt herself gathering for another climax and she moaned. "Come with me. Now."

He thrust into her faster and harder and they exploded together in a burst of sparks and colors. She'd read about things like that before, but had never experienced it. She'd thought it was a myth, she knew better now.

Chapter Eleven

NOLAN WOKE WITH A JOLT, Farley was barking. Nolan got out of bed, pulled on his pants, and slipped on his shoes. Kristen muttered something and he said, "It's okay sweetheart go back to sleep."

He opened the door and quietly called Farley, who came skidding over. He grabbed the keys off the hook by the door and he and Farley went down the outside steps after locking Kristen in safely. They went toward the side of the house where Kristen kept the trashcans. He thought it was probably bears or her raccoon army. He chuckled again at the idea of an army of raccoons. Did they wear camouflage? He imagined a bunch of green-splotched raccoons marching in formation with sniper rifles and hand grenades to raid the garbage.

He and Farley rounded the side of the building and

sure enough, two of the three trash cans were on their sides—one further away from the wall than the other two. He wondered why the third was upside down but assumed Kristen was trying to discourage midnight foragers. Maybe that had ticked off the bears or raccoons. He traced the flashlight around the yard to see if the critters were still hanging around, but decided the dog barking had scared them off.

He put the knocked over trashcans back against the wall, upside down like she had them. He let Farley sniff around and do his business while he looked at the ground for tracks. He didn't see any, but they hadn't had any rain in a while so the ground was hard-packed. Nolan took the long way back to the stairs, just to make sure there wasn't anything else to see.

He thought about the warm, naked woman upstairs in bed and debated going back up to join her. He probably should head on home; it was getting late—or should he say, early. The thought of Kristen all sleepy and relaxed in bed called to him, to rejoin her, but his head convinced him he should go. He didn't want his mother gloating or quizzing him about spending the night. He wondered how long she planned to stay in town. He enjoyed having her, but her visit was definitely hampering, or maybe just changing, his lifestyle.

He hung the keys back on the hook and finished getting dressed. He wrote Kristen a note, and put it on the bed side table. He put the unused condoms in the drawer and then he kissed Kristen. She started to rouse, but he soothed her and told her he needed to go, so she should go back to sleep. He let himself out the door that would lock automatically behind him and went down to his car.

He looked around the yard one more time before he got into the vehicle and drove off. He wondered why the animals were coming so far into town. He should probably ask some of the other people in her neighborhood if they were having trouble, too. It could be the fires sending the animals to lower elevations and into yards looking for food. Yeah, that made sense. Then he laughed at himself—look at the city boy deciding what was normal behavior for animals out in the wilderness. What was he basing his decisions on? Rats and house cats? Some TV show?

One thing he did know was the chemistry between himself and Kristen was off the charts. He'd never been celibate very long, but he'd also never experienced such desire. He couldn't get enough of her—they had slept for an hour or so and then woken to make love twice more. She seemed as greedy for him as he was for her.

He couldn't put his finger on how or why it was different, but it was different. An order of magnitude different or maybe two orders of magnitude. The woman revved him up like he'd never experienced, and the orgasms were so strong he thought they might kill him—so intense and lasted so long. He was getting hard again just thinking about it.

Down boy. No more tonight. But he hoped a repeat would be soon. He just couldn't get enough of her. He was not looking forward to her moving back up the mountain—not that he couldn't drive up there. But it just seemed like a sanctuary on top of the world and he wasn't sure he'd feel welcome.

He wasn't going to buy trouble—there was a lot of summer and warm fall to get through before they would see the first snowfall. All the experts said the forest fires would probably continue until snow covered the whole area. He wondered why rain wouldn't do it. He had a lot to learn about living in a small town out in the middle of nowhere. Animal habits, forest fire indicators, tourist flow, small town idiosyncrasies—well, he had plenty of time. He planned to be here for a long while.

Chapter Twelve

KRISTEN WOKE THE NEXT MORNING very relaxed and a little achy, but it was the best kind of sore. She vaguely remembered Nolan leaving, as if in a dream. But he was clearly gone, so it must have been real. On the night stand was a note from him. How sweet was that? She was a little disappointed he hadn't stayed, but at the same time, she wasn't sure she was ready to announce their change in relationship to the world—so maybe it was for the better. The note mentioned her trash being knocked over again which seemed kind of odd since it was empty. In her experience, animals didn't come around unless there was something to attract them. Some nice, smelly garbage for instance.

Kristen sat up in bed and looked around. Nolan had picked up her clothes and laid them neatly on the chair she had in the corner. Farley was in his dog bed by the fireplace, which wasn't needed in the summer; she wondered if it worked. She probably wouldn't still be here in the winter, but it would be a good idea to have someone come check and make sure the fireplaces wouldn't be a fire hazard to use.

Her bedroom was a pleasant space someone had renovated to make larger. It looked like two small rooms had been combined to create a pleasant, large space with a walk-in closet and attached bath. Definitely not a typical design in a Victorian house. There were two small bedrooms with a bath in between them across the hall, so a nice family-of-four house. The other side on this floor held a kitchen and living room. Above was the attic, which was divided into storage space and another room—she imagined an office would be nice up there or maybe an exercise area.

Farley woke up and came over to see if she was going to let him out. She put on yoga pants and a tank top—it was already heating up for the day. Fall wasn't far away, but it was still warm in the late summer and the sun was brightly shining. She put coffee on before going downstairs to let Farley out. As she waited for him she wondered what kind of hours she should open the gallery and what she should name it. Mary Ann could work part of the time, but should she hire someone for weekends. So many questions! She should probably talk to Barbara and her partners to see what kind of hours were popular, since they had the business next door. Chris would be good to ask about hiring people, a business license, and some of those details.

She called Farley to get him to come in—she needed caffeine. He usually came right back, but he must have found something interesting to investigate. He came around from the side of the house where she kept the trash. She took him in to give him some breakfast and herself some liquid energy.

Farley wolfed down his food—like normal—while she sat at the table, drank her coffee, and checked her email, website, and then Facebook. She'd sold some things at the gallery in Wenatchee and they had added the money to her PayPal account. They also asked for a few new items. She had an email from a high school friend, Shelly, who now lived in Colorado asking for a bracelet to match the pendant and earrings she'd made her. She did have some blue topaz stones that she'd kind of set aside for Shelly thinking she might like something new. She would work up a design and send it to her. Vangie emailed to say she had gotten the last piece she'd made for her and worn it to a family reunion. Everyone had raved about it, so Vangie was on cloud nine.

Farley started whining at the door to be let out, which was odd—they'd only been back in the house maybe an hour. But he was a well-behaved dog, so she knew there must be a reason. She took him back downstairs and let him out. He ran over to the side of the yard and started throwing up. What was that all about? She went over to see what was going on and he dropped to his belly. Then he got back up and threw up again. This was not good. She better call the vet and have him checked out. Damn, her phone was upstairs. She left Farley laying in the yard and ran up to get her phone. When she got back down, her poor dog was still laying in a boneless heap.

She quickly dialed the vet in Chelan—they didn't have one in their tiny town of Chedwick. The vet made some suggestions and told her if he wasn't better this afternoon to bring him on the ferry into the office. If she called him first, he'd keep the clinic open and wait for her. She hoped it didn't come to that, but she wouldn't hesitate if he wasn't better by then. If he got any worse, she could take the fast ferry that only ran in the summer for quick trips up lake. First order from the vet was water, so he wouldn't dehydrate. She coaxed Farley to follow her into the house and gave him fresh water in his bowl.

She wondered if his delay this morning had been from him eating something in the yard that had disagreed with him. The vet had suggested chicken broth or something with electrolytes like Pedialyte or Gatorade. She didn't have anything like that in the house, so she called the little store in town and they assured her they had some, but they couldn't spare anyone to bring it over. She decided to call Barbara and then remembered she was filling in today at the amusement park. Terry and Greg were fishing. Mary Ann didn't answer her phone, which was very odd—she usually answered on the first ring. She decided to call Nolan and see if he'd do it. She didn't want to call him, but she was getting desperate and she didn't want to leave Farley in case he got worse.

She bit her lip in indecision and then called him before she could change her mind. Her dog needed her.

"Hi, Kristen."

"Nolan, can you do me a huge favor?"

"Yes. What is it?"

"Would you go to the market and pick up the items they have ready for me?"

"Sure. Do you need it right away?"

"Yes, please," she said with a small hitch in her voice.

"I'll be there soon."

NOLAN RAN UP THE back stairs and knocked on the door. The items in Kristen's bags were very odd so he wondered what was going on.

She answered the door and dragged him inside. "You're here. That was fast. Thanks so much. I don't know. I don't know what to do first. What to give him first. Maybe I should call back."

Nolan took her by the arms and looked her in the eye. "Calm down, breathe, and tell me what's wrong."

"Farley. He's sick. He never gets sick. I fed him and then he threw it all up. I called the vet and he said to give him water and electrolytes and bring him in if he wasn't better. He's been asleep ever since. I brought him in and he drank some water and then fell asleep."

"Okay. Now relax, sweetheart. Dogs sometimes eat things they shouldn't and throw up. He was just sick once right?"

"Yes. I fed him and he ate like normal, but then a little while later he started whining to go out. When I let him out, he ran across the yard and then threw up several times and then I brought him in and he drank some water and fell asleep."

"That doesn't sound too bad, if it was just him getting rid of his breakfast. Any idea what might have caused it?"

Kristen shook her head. "When I let him out this morning, he didn't come back right away like he normally does, and I had to call him back. So, I don't know if he ate something while he was out of sight. He was over by the trash, but I know the cans were empty."

"Yeah, they were, but something might have fallen out and then got rotten."

"Maybe. Let's give him the no-flavor Pedialyte mixed with some beef broth and see how that goes down."

Nolan mixed up the concoction while Kristen cleaned out his food bowl just in case there was something bad in it. Then she washed out the water bowl, too, and refilled it with clean water. Kristen called Farley in and he did drink both the broth and some water. He went over to Nolan for a good rub and wagged his tail.

"He seems better," she said with a small catch in her voice.

"I think he'll be fine. But you, I'm not so sure of."

Kristen tried to blink back her tears.

Nolan took her by the hand, sat down, pulled her onto his lap, and held her while she cried. He ran his hand up and down her back and muttered nonsense to soothe her. Farley came over, sat down next to her, and put his head on her knee.

She laughed through her tears at her dog trying to comfort her. She patted his head and then she said to him, "I'm okay, but I don't want you to do that again. No more eating junk in the yard. Do you understand me?"

Farley whined and Kristen laughed. Nolan smiled and decided they were all going to be fine.

Nolan stayed and they both kept an eye on Farley who seemed to be doing better by the hour. He drank more of the Pedialyte and beef broth mixture and water. When he only continued to improve, Kristen called the vet in Chelan to tell him he was doing fine and they wouldn't be bringing him on the late ferry. The vet recommended starting him back on bland foods like white chicken meat with some slippery elm, which was a natural herb that helped with digestive issues. Later tonight would be fine, as long as he kept getting better. He said to give Farley just a small portion and then wait an hour or so to make sure it stayed down and then she could give him a bit more.

WHEN IT APPEARED THE crisis had passed Kristen realized she was famished and since Nolan had spent the whole day with her, she knew he must be hungry, too.

"You've been here all day. Are you starving? I am."

"I could eat," he said.

"Oh, my God, look at me. I'm still in my yoga pants and tank top from this morning. I didn't even shower. I probably smell and look like crap."

"Not that I noticed. I think you look kind of hot," Nolan said.

She groaned. "Just like a man, if it shows off the curves you're happy."

"Well, duh. I like looking at your curves. And kissing them. And tasting them. And running my hands over them."

Kristen felt her face get hot. "Enough of that talk. I was going to offer to feed you."

"I could get on board with that idea…or we could go back to your room for more sex. I think there's another strip of condoms we didn't use last night."

"Um, food. I want to keep an eye on Farley."

"Damn, want me to order something? You could shower and change if you want, while I wait for delivery."

"So, I do smell and look like crap."

Nolan laughed. "No, silly. Didn't I just tell you I thought you looked hot? But if it'll make you feel better to shower, I'm willing to keep an eye on Farley while you do."

"Well, in that case, I'll take you up on the offer."

"Good. Does anyone else in town deliver beside the pizza place?"

"No not really, but pizza is a favorite of mine, just don't get peppers—they don't like me. Anything else is fine, except anchovies."

He asked, "Meat lovers?"

"Perfect. Maybe with olives so we get a veggie in there, too."

"Good. Now, you go on. Don't hurry—we've got plenty of time."

Nolan called in the order and waited for the delivery which was pretty quick, about a half hour. He paid the delivery guy, took the pizza into the kitchen, and nearly dropped it on the floor when Kristen came into the room. She had on the shortest shorts he'd seen since the Dukes of Hazzard. They were white denim and showed off her tanned legs. Her top was red and had ruffles around the neck. It was a soft-looking material and it was sleeveless. She'd put her hair up with little bits of it hanging down caressing her neck and shoulders. And she'd put on makeup or something that made her eyes all dark and smoky and her mouth red and wet. Shit, he didn't want to eat pizza— he wanted to kiss those lips and lick everywhere else starting with her neck and work his way down. Then he would run his hands over her arms and legs. And....

"Oh, good. Food. I'm starving! Let's eat."

Dragging his mind out of the gutter, he said, "Right, eat. I got out some plates and stuff."

"Mmm. You did good. Beer and pizza—what more could a girl ask for?"

Nolan had some ideas, but decided to keep them to himself—at least until she'd eaten.

Kristen grabbed two pieces of pizza and a beer and sat down at the table. Farley came over and put his head on her knee.

"Since he's begging for pizza I think his stomach must be feeling better." She looked at him. "Thanks for coming over to help. You didn't question me, you just came over and spent the whole day."

He smiled. "I enjoy spending time with you and I've noticed you only ask for help when you really need it, so why would I question you?"

"Well, I appreciate it—and this pizza." She took a big bite and groaned, which made Nolan think about other ways to make her moan. Food. He needed to eat, not think about sex. Food.

Chapter Thirteen

KRISTEN STOPPED MID BITE. The pizza hung in the air about to drip cheese and sauce and meat all over. "Hey, where's your mom? You haven't even called her, have you?"

"No. She was up last night—or rather this morning. She got inspiration for a new piece. Which means she'll be drawing it over and over for at least two days. She won't know if I'm home or not. She probably won't eat much or sleep. When she gets it perfect, she'll eat and then sleep for about twenty-four hours." He shrugged. "Then she'll want to get started creating—it's my guess she'll leave and go back home. My stuff might be here by that time, but even if I got it set up for her to use, it wouldn't be as good as the setup she has at home. She'll be busy creating it for a week or two. But during that time, she will only eat and sleep between each phase of the creation."

"So, you've been through this a time or two, have you?"

"Ever since I was a baby. She hired nannies for us when we were little, so that we were taken care of. And my father wasn't an artist, so he kept regular hours. How do you operate?"

"I don't do real long creative sessions. Since everything I'm doing is very tiny, both my eyes and hands need rest. I might go for an eight-hour stretch of working, but I can't do days on end like your mom. And I work on a dozen pieces or more at a time. Some are at the same place in the design, so I can do a little assembly line. But then I will also have some that are completely different, so I don't get bored doing all the same thing.

"I might have a half-dozen pair of identical earrings I'm doing, while at the same time working on three very different pendants and three rings. Some are commission pieces and some are stock to place in galleries. And then there are the never-ending charms. Thank God, I finally farmed some of that work out to other people in town. After making the same thing a hundred thousand times, I want to melt them all into a little pile of metal and never look at them again. But of course, I refrain—since they very nicely pay the bills."

Nolan nodded. "But you actually keep living your life, even during a creative jag."

"Yes. I eat and sleep and walk my dog and answer email and get on Facebook. When I'm up on the mountain

I don't do a lot of socializing, but I talk to my sister and other friends in town, so I'm not a complete recluse."

"Since you've been in town you've had a lot of interaction with people. Is it bothering you?"

"No, not really. Your mom and Mary Ann have helped. They've met with the artists bringing in their work and left me alone to keep working. So, surprisingly enough, it's actually been easier than I feared."

Just then the fire siren started blaring. Kristen jumped. "Oh, I'm not used to hearing that. I wonder what it is."

"You are probably the only person in town without a fire scanner."

"I normally live too far away to be a volunteer myself. I'll probably need to get a scanner now that I'm a business owner, so that if any of the volunteers are in my gallery when the siren goes off, they will know what they need to do."

"I'm going to call the dispatcher and find out what's happening in case they need some police backup. They'll call me if…" Nolan was cut off when his phone rang and it was the dispatcher. "Officer Thompson." Nolan listened to the dispatcher.

"Yes. I'll be right there. I'm not in uniform, but I have a police jacket in the car I can put on. Ten minutes." He hung up and looked at Kristen. "There is a giant fire in the field behind the fire chief's house. It can be seen all over town and they need police backup to keep people out of the way. I need to go."

"Of course. Be safe."

"I will. Have a good night," he said and gave her a smacking kiss on her lips and hustled out the door.

Kristen looked out the door in the direction of the fire chief's house and she could see the glow and occasional bursts of flames. She hoped the firefighters on the mountain didn't get worried. Of course, the dispatcher was probably in communication with the hotshots.

NOLAN PUT THE portable light on the top of his civilian car and turned it on, so he could get close to the fire's command area. He got out of the vehicle and put on the police jacket he always kept in his car. He spotted the chief of police and went over to see where they wanted him.

James McGregor turned toward him with a smirk on his lips. "Ah, Officer Nolan. Good of you to come in. It's a large fire and can be seen from a long distance. We had calls from people on their house boats out in the lake and some of the people on the ridge in Mason could see it— even the forest fire fighters called in to ask if we needed assistance. But the only thing burning is a very large brush pile and it's pretty isolated, other than an old chicken coop near it. Wouldn't hurt if that burned down too."

"How did it get started?"

"No one's saying, but the teenage daughter of the fire chief and her boyfriend are looking a little apprehensive. I've heard the chief mention it would be handy if it burned down, but I can't say he'd actually sanction such behavior."

"So, are they going to investigate?"

"No, I think we'll just chalk it up to fireworks."

"Fireworks? It's not exactly the Fourth of July."

"No, it's not—but it's also just a bunch of old tree branches. Let's think of it as a large bonfire."

"A bonfire without a permit, sir."

"Welcome to Small Town, USA, Nolan. Now, how about you go over there and keep the look-e-loos out of the way of the fire fighters. They're just going to let it burn itself out unless conditions change. But it's a still night and we don't expect any trouble."

Nolan just shook his head. Welcome to Small Town, USA, indeed. Deliberate arson by the fire chief's daughter and her boyfriend—who is a volunteer firefighter—and they are going to put down fireworks as the cause. Incredible, but he had to admit it made him feel a little nostalgic for the past and the way the world used to be run. Anywhere else, the girl and her boyfriend would be spending the night in jail.

He got over to the area he was supposed to be watching and without even saying a word to them, everyone backed up to where he'd have directed them. Nolan shook his head over the crowd obedience and texted Kristen to let her know what was going on, adding his astonishment over the way they were treating it. She just LOLed him and texted welcome to the boonies.

AFTER NOLAN TEXTED her about the fire, Kristen decided to see if she could get a little work done. It wasn't real late and she'd lost the whole day to Farley being sick. She normally worked six or more hours on a Saturday. Too tired from all their activity last night she probably wouldn't stay up that late, but she could easily get in two or three hours and make it to bed at a reasonable time. The gallery in Leavenworth was asking for a half-dozen earrings sets, so she could work on those. They were at the stage of adding fresh water pearls to hang in the center. They were a moon shaped and had copper and silver textured metal with a dangling pearl. Each batch she made had the same design but when she did a new set she'd change it up a little, so that there were small differences between the groups. It made life more interesting and that also kept them unique for the buyer. They wouldn't find the same earrings on more than a dozen people. Of course, since they were handmade—rather than stamped out by a machine—the earrings in a set would not be exactly identical.

She kept Farley with her while she worked, still wanting to keep an eye on him. He'd eaten a small amount of his regular dog food and he seemed to be fine. She shook her head, he just must have gotten into something that disagreed with him—probably some old garbage or even a dead animal. Yucky, but entirely possible.

Chapter Fourteen

MONDAY, WHEN MARY ANN walked into the shop, she had the goofiest grin on her face Kristen had ever seen. "Oh, my God. You got laid, didn't you."

"Yes, I did. All weekend, and it was glorious."

"All weekend?"

"All. Weekend. Friday night. Saturday. Sunday. All. Weekend."

Kristen crossed her arms across her chest in mock severity. "Well, rub it in. I only got Friday night."

"What? You and Nolan did the nasty? You go, girl."

Kristen blushed. "Yes, but we didn't do marathon. Just a few times on Friday."

"A few times?"

"Um, well, yeah. He did wear me out a little."

"Good for him. The boy has stamina, does he?"

"Cops and firefighters *have* to have stamina."

Mary Ann hooted. "Yes, they do—and lucky for us."

Kristen chuckled. "Someone needs to appreciate—all that nice, hard...stamina."

"Oh, you are so bad."

"Okay, enough of this. Let's get busy before the parade of people start up today. Oh, Nolan said he'd come by after his shift to get the equipment from your house."

"Good. So, what do you want to work on today?"

"I worked on these earrings on Saturday night during the unsanctioned bonfire, and decided this might be a good item to get you started on. Since they can all be a little different they would also be a good place for you to try a bit of creativity. I sell a lot of them, so they are always in demand and I don't like all the different batches to be exactly the same, so you could play around with them while using the basic design that people really like."

"Oh goody. I'd love to do them. They don't look real complex."

"No, so let me show you how I do them with the first pair, then you can make up some of your own."

Kristen showed Mary Ann the way to create them and then let her try it out, while Kristen worked on several rings she'd started for three different clients. She also had an earring that had some fire scale along the top that she needed to buff out. Silver liked to turn colors when it was heated and the impurities came out, but it didn't look so pretty on a finished piece. The boric acid and denatured alcohol mixture she always put on silver usually took care of the problem, but this time it hadn't, so it would take some elbow grease to get it off.

Mary Ann was having so much fun with the earrings that when the doorbell to the main house rang in the shop, Kristen let her keep working and went to answer the summons. On the porch was a delivery, but the guy wasn't familiar to Kristen, so she wondered what he was bringing.

"I have a delivery for Kristen Matthews."

"That's me."

"Can I see some ID please."

"Really?"

"Yes, I can only deliver it to Kristen Matthews and I must verify identity."

"Okay, it will take me a minute."

"That's fine I'll bring the packages up to the porch."

Kristen was confused. Packages? Confirm identity? What kind of delivery service was this? By the time she got to the door, she'd decided she was going to find out, before she let this guy leave strange boxes.

She opened the door and there he was with a half dozen large parcels lined up. Stranger and stranger. "So, can you please tell me who these packages are coming from?"

"Yes, ma'am, as soon as I see your ID."

Kristen showed him her ID and he said in an almost hushed voice, "These are from Lucille Thompson. They are insured for a half million dollars."

"Oh, well, that makes sense, but that seems like a huge responsibility."

"Yes, ma'am and as soon as I get them in the door, they will be *your* responsibility."

Oh, dear God. Her responsibility? She was going to call Nolan ASAP and find out what to do with them—she was afraid to even open them.

"Please bring them in and I'll show you where to put them." She led the way to the part of the gallery where they had decided Lucille's work should be displayed. He very carefully put each box down and went back for the others. As soon as he'd set them down and left, she called Nolan.

"Your mother just had a half million dollars' worth of her art delivered. I'm afraid to look at the boxes, let alone open them." She said before he could even say hello.

"Oh, I thought she said she was sending a million dollars' worth."

"What? Is she crazy?"

"Not at all, is there only three boxes then?"

"No, there are six."

"Oh, then it's all there."

"A million dollars' worth?" Kristen felt like she was going to faint or throw up or wet her pants.

"Yeah. Oh, the delivery guy told you a half million, didn't he? That's just how much she insures it for, not the value."

"Oh, my God, Nolan! That scares the ever living shit out of me. Couldn't she have sent her inexpensive art?"

Nolan chuckled. "Kristen, that *is* her inexpensive art."

"Oh, no. Really? I think I'm going to throw up."

"Don't be silly, if you are really scared to open the boxes, I'll help you when I get Mary Ann's equipment from her house."

"Okay, good. That way if we break them it will be her son's fault."

"She hasn't left town yet. When I go home after work to change, I'll see if she's available to come too."

"Even better. Thanks." Not at all relieved, she peered at the boxes, but didn't go near them. A million dollars of glass art in her gallery. What in the hell was going on here? She didn't want responsibility for that kind of money.

Mary Ann walked in. "You didn't come back. What's wrong? You look like you've seen a ghost."

"Not a ghost. Just a million dollars in art."

Mary Ann clapped her hands. "Oh goody, Lucille's art came. Let's open it."

Kristen nearly shouted, "Oh, hell no! We are not going to open it. Not until Nolan or Lucille—or preferably both—are here. You knew she was sending a million dollars of art?"

"Yes, of course. She told me all about the pieces she was sending." Mary Ann nodded.

"But a million dollars…"

Mary Ann shrugged. "What did you think she was going to send?"

"I don't know, but I didn't think it would be that much. That's like a hundred and fifty thousand each." Kristen huffed.

"Yes, it is. And her art is worth every penny. In fact, that's kind of low for her art, it must be some smaller pieces."

"But who will buy it?"

Mary Ann snorted. "Oh, you just get the word out that you have her art in your little gallery here and you'll have plenty of people coming to buy it. Tourist problems are going to be a thing of the past, my friend. In fact, you better get some high-end jewelry ready for those rich people to buy. That three-thousand-dollar pendant of yours will be a drop in the bucket."

Kristen sat down, right on the floor, in the middle of the showroom. "I don't think I can handle this."

Mary Ann sat next to her and took one of Kristen's cold hands and started rubbing it to bring the warmth back. "It will be just fine, don't worry."

Kristen laid down on the floor and laughed a little hysterically. "Right. Just fine."

NOLAN WAS GLAD he didn't have too much longer on his shift. Kristen had sounded a little freaked out. He guessed she didn't work in art that was so high priced, but his mother's creations weren't cheap. The pieces she had sent Kristen did indicate that his mother had confidence in the gallery and even the town. His mother didn't put her sculptures just anywhere.

Nolan met Mary Ann at her house. "So, how is Kristen? Is she still freaked out?"

"She's not laying in the middle of the showroom floor anymore, so that must mean she's better. She grew up pretty poor, so I think the idea of that much money is overwhelming."

"Let's get this stuff loaded, so we can get over there. Mom is going to meet us in a half hour or so. She was just getting up after sleeping for a whole day, so food and company sounded good to her. I called Amber and she's making us up some dinner. She even volunteered to deliver it because she wants to see my mom's art. It's a slow night at her place, so she can get away."

"Oh goody! An unveiling party." Mary Ann grinned.

Nolan laughed. "Yeah, I guess it is."

KRISTEN KNEW MARY Ann and Nolan would be there soon. She put Farley upstairs in their living space, so he wouldn't run in and out while they were carrying in the equipment. She didn't want him loose when they opened Lucille's glass work, either. Not that he was a bad dog, but he did get happy to see his friends and that tail could wreak havoc. She put on some lip-gloss, a spritz of perfume, and fluffed her hair. She wasn't primping for the man, just looking nice. Yeah, right. She didn't lie to herself and she wasn't going to start now. She was *totally* primping. She was a woman and she could fuss if she wanted to.

She heard a car door shut and went downstairs to open up. Nolan was carrying in the buffer and Mary Ann was carrying in some of the smaller things.

Nolan smiled at her and winked. "Here I am to help you unpack my mom's stuff. She'll be over in a bit; she was just going to shower, after sleeping around the clock. Amber is going to bring some food, too. She wanted to see the art."

"Great. That sounds like fun."

Nolan, Kristen, and Mary Ann got the little workroom all set up. It didn't have a lot of space, but it would be enough to work on some things while waiting for gallery customers. They set it up so it was efficient and cozy, with plastic walls to keep the buffing compound from spreading. Lucille and Amber got there about the same time, so they decided to eat before they unpacked the art.

While they were eating, Mayor Carol came in. "I heard you got Lucille's art today, so I wanted to come see."

"Great to have you, Mayor," Kristen said graciously.

Kyle and Samantha came in a few minutes later. "Hey, we came to see the show. And Samantha brought pie for after."

Barbara, Chris, Greg and Terry came in next. Followed by Jeremy.

Dear God, was the whole town coming? Kristen looked around and wondered who was next. It was Gus with his camera—he planned to write up an article for the paper, and also wanted to put some information about the gallery into the brochure he was designing.

Gus said, "And ya should put up a website ta advertise. With Mrs. Thompson's work, you'll draw in tourists with big money. Good thinking, Kristen."

Kristen just smiled. She hadn't been thinking about it at all. In fact, this whole thing was not her idea. He'd railroaded her into it and now it had taken on a life of its own, and she was just trying to keep up. Trying and failing.

Lucille beamed. "Please call me Lucille, Gus—and I do hope you're right, and my art is a draw for people to come and enjoy your town. Let's get them opened, shall we? Nolan, you know how they're packed. Will you do the honors?"

"Yes. I brought some tools with me." He moved to the first box and cut it open with a box cutter.

Kristen was surprised to see a custom wooden crate, surrounded by packing peanuts, inside the cardboard box. Nolan had to use a small crowbar to get the top off the crate. Inside there were more peanuts and a wooden frame with foam rubber attached, holding the glass piece at all the critical points of stress. Nolan carefully detached the supports. The last thing left was a film covering the piece to protect the glass surface from scratches. When that was finally peeled off everyone gasped at the beauty of the piece. Kristen realized the whole crowd had been holding their breath as each new layer of protection was removed.

Lucille and Mary Ann directed Nolan where they wanted the sculpture placed and the whole process began again. It took a couple hours to get them all unpacked, arranged, and exclaimed over.

When the last one was settled Samantha said, "Now, let's celebrate with pie. I brought cherry and blueberry."

No one turned down the pie.

Samantha had even brought plates, napkins, and forks so they didn't need to leave the room and could enjoy the gallery acquisitions as they ate. As Samantha dished up the dessert, everyone pitched in to clean up the wrappings. There were bags and bags of packing peanuts. Kristen wondered if the post office in town could use them. She'd be happy to donate them—then again, what if she had to ship Lucille's art? She would need to repack them back the way they had come. Well, Nolan was just going to have to help with that.

As they ate the pastry they wandered from area to area, looking at all the different items that had been put out. Kristen wandered too, and was surprised when she came upon some very good wood carvings. The tag said Tim Jefferson.

Kristen went over to Mary Ann. "I had no idea we had wood carvings from Tim Jefferson in our mix."

"Yes. He brought them in and asked if they were good enough to put in the gallery. Lucille was here at the time and we both told him they were excellent. He told us a story about how Ellen had given him his first good adult pocket knife, when he was ten years old. At their first Christmas together, before she and Hank got married. He said it was his most prized possession and he'd worn it out with carving."

"That's awesome. We should have Gus write that up for his brochure—that's the kind of stories that draw people."

"He said he has hundreds of carvings. He wanted to sell them for ten dollars each, but Lucille said they were worth way more than that. So, he agreed to let her price them. He didn't even stay to see what price she put on them, but said to call him when we need more."

"Really? That is so cool. Gus, come over here, Mary Ann has a story to tell you." Kristen left Mary Ann to relate the story and went back to look at the carvings.

There were about two dozen and they were extremely varied in subject matter. There were old men and children and cowboys and military men. There were horses and bears and chipmunks. There were lions and giraffes and elephants. There were houses and cottages and tents. There were famous landmarks like the Eiffel Tower, the Golden Gate Bridge, and the Seattle Space Needle. It was amazing. He was very talented. She guessed he was about twenty years old now. If they got some people into the gallery, he was going to be a rich young man.

Mary Ann came up to Kristen. "So, are we open for business? Several people have asked me if they can buy things."

"Really? Well, I guess so. I think all the paperwork is complete. We have the scanner for credit cards, and we could take cash or checks and just put them in a drawer or something."

"Good." Mary Ann raised her voice, "Kristen says we're legal to sell, so anyone who wants to, can buy things tonight."

Nearly everyone bought something. Gus bought one of the glass sculptures for two hundred thousand dollars. Greg bought a woodcarving of a bear standing on its hind legs. Chris bought Barbara some earrings and a necklace to match. Barbara bought one of Jeremy's storybooks and one of the hand painted toys Greg had done, for the baby on the way—and on it went. When everyone was finished purchasing, there was a quarter million dollars in sales and they weren't even open yet!

Lucille laughed. "I guess I better get some more stock on its way here. I'm going to leave tomorrow, to go back home—I need to work on my new idea."

Everyone was sad to see her go and told her they hoped she'd be back soon. She assured them she would be.

They all started drifting out, until there was only Kristen, Mary Ann, and Nolan left.

Nolan looked around. "So, it looks like this is going to be a success. When do you plan to open officially?"

"I guess it better be soon." Kristen frowned. "I probably should have some kind of open house or grand opening. Maybe next week."

"Maybe we should plan for Friday—we can get in some snacks from Samantha's bakery, let the other towns on the lake know. Maybe even put some ads in the papers in Leavenworth and Wenatchee," Mary Ann said.

"Good ideas. We can have a few drawings throughout the day for small items. Maybe do an opening day twenty-percent-off-all-purchases thing."

Nolan shook his head. "Ten percent off is enough. You still have to pay your artisans and make money. You are going to have operating costs that you aren't used to paying for. So, you need to get in the black as quickly as possible. Have you hired any help besides Mary Ann?"

"No, not really. I have a couple of other people who do some of the finishing work for me. I haven't talked to any of them about coming in and manning the gallery. But I need to—Mary Ann and I can't run it seven days a week. I think it should be open from eleven in the morning until about eight at night, so that's nine hours. I could use maybe two more people—one that wants to work evenings and one or two for weekends. It might be good to have overlap on weekends when we might be busier."

Mary Ann shuffled her feet. "I mentioned the gallery to Tammy O'Conner. She said she'd love to work in it on the weekends in the morning, before Jeff goes to Greg's, that way he could watch the little ones. I hope you don't mind me telling her about it."

"Not at all. I think that would be a great idea—she'd also be good for school days during school hours as backup. I'll call her tomorrow. Any other suggestions?"

"Not right off the top of my head, but I'll think about it."

"Good. Now, you've been here all day—go home and relax."

Mary Ann saluted. "Yes, ma'am."

Nolan watched Mary Ann leave and looked at Kristen. "She's quite an asset. Have you thought about making her a partner in the gallery?"

Kristen looked back at him, her mouth agape. "No, I haven't—and that is a great idea. I hope she'll be doing most of the management, so she *should* be a partner. She's got a good head on her shoulders. I'll talk to her about it tomorrow. So, do you want to come up for a night cap, or something?"

"I'd love to, but since mom is leaving in the morning, I think I should be a good son and go spend the rest of the time she's here with her. Can I take a rain check?"

"Sure. It was lovely meeting her, and obviously, her art in our little gallery is going to be a major contributor. Thanks for everything you did tonight. I really appreciate it."

"My pleasure. How about a little goodbye kiss?"

"That would be *my* pleasure." And she walked into his arms.

Chapter Fifteen

THE NEXT ELEVEN DAYS WERE a whirlwind of activity. Mary Ann gladly accepted the partnership and dug into organizing the grand opening with gusto. She still checked with Kristen on everything, but her confidence really soared. They spent mornings in the studio— Kristen worked on her commissions and some new, more expensive pieces for the gallery and Mary Ann produced some of the easier items. She encouraged Mary Ann to try out her own ideas. Reasoning that if Mary Ann had some of her own designs in the gallery it would give her a greater sense of ownership.

In the afternoons, Mary Ann worked on the grand opening and talking to various townspeople who might be interested in a part time job in the gallery. So many people worked in the amusement park that it wasn't an easy task to find helpers. Mary Ann had called several people, but wasn't having a lot of luck—she still needed someone for evenings and someone for weekend afternoons.

One afternoon Kristen was startled by Mary Ann crashing into the studio. "What the hell? Is something wrong?"

"No, sorry. I was just so excited I had to come tell you. Tim Jefferson called, and asked if he could work evenings!"

"Yay?" Kristen wondered what the big deal was.

"I have been having so much trouble trying to find someone to work evenings—almost everyone is working at the amusement park now. I felt like doing cartwheels when he called, but instead I calmly asked him to please come in for an interview. He agreed to come in on Tuesday before the grand opening. Isn't that wonderful? He asked if he could come in after five, because he has to finish up his day at the ranch. I told him that would be fine, is it okay with you?"

Kristen smiled. "Tuesday is great. I'd like to talk to him about his art, too. I think he'd be an asset, if he doesn't have that silent, brooding, cowboy thing going on."

"Yeah, that wouldn't work too well in the gallery. I still need someone for weekend evenings."

Kristen said, "I can do that until we find someone. I should probably spend some time in the gallery—at least while we are just getting started."

"It wouldn't be too much?"

"I wouldn't want to do it forever, but a few weeks or a month or two would be okay."

Mary Ann sighed. "If you're certain—that would give me a little more time to look around. And it would let me work on the grand opening more."

"Yes, I can do it for a while."

Mary Ann grinned. "Yay! But right now, I better get back over there." And she charged back out the door, leaving Kristen feeling like a whirlwind had just left. Mary Ann was certainly having fun.

NOLAN SPENT HIS days investigating a rash of small burglaries that were taking place. A few businesses had called in, saying that they had found an ajar door or window and had some small, easy to carry items taken from their stores. One or two also reported cash missing. Some owners were a little lax about security measures. Since it was a small town, Nolan understood the mentality of trusting neighbors. But he tried to convince those proprietors that with the larger tourist influx for the summer it would be wise to invest in more security—even if it was just a safe to put their cash in each day.

Everyone on the police force thought it looked like the same person burglarizing the businesses. There was never any damage to the stores and the amounts stolen were always small—only misdemeanors. Usually, the entry was a window that had been left open for the cool summer breezes.

Nolan decided he should go by the gallery and see if Kristen had done anything about security before she officially opened on Friday. She'd put the money and checks into an envelope the night of the impromptu opening, so he wanted to make sure she'd progressed from that practice. He decided to go by after work, even though he wanted to talk to her in an official capacity. He could spend more time with her once he was finished for the day.

He found both Kristen and Mary Ann in the gallery showing Tim Jefferson around.

Kristen's eyes lit up when he walked in. "Nolan, welcome. We're just showing our new evening employee around."

"Tim, welcome to the best art gallery in town." Nolan shook Tim's hand.

Kristen laughed. "Easy for you to say, since it's also the only art gallery in town."

"It would be the best, even if there were a dozen others." Nolan lifted one shoulder in a half shrug.

Mary Ann grinned at him and said to Tim, "Come with me, let me show you the last area while Kristen talks to Nolan."

"Actually, the first order of business involves all of you. I wanted to come by to ask you about security measures for the gallery. We've had a string of small burglaries in town at some of the local businesses. Most of them have just had a few small items stolen."

Mary Ann nodded. "I have heard something about that."

Nolan continued, "So I wanted to come by to see if you have gotten a safe for your daily sales or if you have a security system. Also, most—if not all—of the break-ins have been through an open window. So, I wanted to warn you to make sure your windows are all closed and locked. We're trying to talk to all the businesses to give them a heads-up."

"We did order a safe today, after Mary Ann heard about the burglaries, but it won't be here until late next week," Kristen said. "I suppose we should get some kind of alarm system, besides Farley barking. Lucille's sculptures alone are reason enough for that."

"They are expensive, but they would be cumbersome to steal and almost impossible to sell, unless the thief had a buyer beforehand. This particular thief seems to take smaller items that are not too unique. He or she doesn't seem to be out for big ticket items—just small, easy to transport things."

"Oh, like my jewelry?"

"Maybe, but even that is pretty unique, isn't it?" Nolan asked.

Kristen nodded. "Yes, but I make some things in quantity."

"Nothing taken so far has been unique. He or she would have to be pretty familiar with your art to know which were which. But regardless, you might want to consider an alarm system. There are several companies in Wenatchee that could do it."

"Okay, Mary Ann or I will call them tomorrow. You

know I really hate all this. It's part of the reason I live on top of a mountain. I don't have to be worried about thieves and security and bad guys. I just have bears or raccoon armies who only want my trash—not my hard-earned money. Although, I do have to keep shiny items out of sight, because raccoons love shiny things."

Mary Ann shook her head. "Come on, Tim. Let me show you the rest and then we can get out of here. See you tomorrow, Kristen."

Tim blinked. "Oh, okay. Thanks for the job, Kristen. I'm looking forward to working here." He nodded at Nolan. "Officer Thompson."

Nolan smiled warmly at Kristen. "I take it Mary Ann has heard that rant before."

"I suppose, but it is how I feel." Kristen sighed.

A shadow crossed his eyes. "I know. Injustice and the inability to be safe is the reason I became a police officer."

Kristen remembered all his mother had told her and nodded, trying to keep her expression blank. He had been through a lot harder issues than she had.

Nolan brightened. "I did come by to tell you all those things, which I could have done while on duty, but I decided to wait so we could hang out a bit. Maybe go get some dinner at Amber's. Interested?"

"Hanging out, absolutely. Dinner at Amber's? Not so much. How about we grill some meat, bake a potato or two and stay in? All this *being with people all the time* doesn't entice me to go out."

"Oh, well, if you would rather be alone...."

"Didn't say that. I just would rather be with you. Alone. Without others. Might want to get you naked later."

"I could get on board with that."

Kristen smirked. "I thought that might be the case. Let's go get some food started."

"The naked could come first, if you want."

"No, we should eat first—so we have energy for the naked."

Nolan followed Kristen up the stairs, muttering, "Power bars are good for energy. Granola bars are good for energy. Candy bars are good for energy."

Kristen just laughed at him.

They worked together getting dinner ready. Nolan manned the grill while Kristen made cheesy mashed potatoes and a salad. Farley kept Nolan company outside near the meat. Nolan slipped him a small snack of the beef. He almost got caught feeding the dog people-food when Kristen stuck her head out to ask if he wanted to eat on the deck.

He hollered back, "Sure, I'll come up and carry some stuff down as soon as I turn the meat over." Looking at Farley. "No more for you, we almost got caught on that last one."

Farley sighed and went to lay down in the shade of the tree, which had become his personal space. Nolan brought down the plates, silverware, salad dressing, and a couple of beers.

When the grilling was done, Kristen carried the potatoes and salad down. It was a nice night for it, with the sun getting ready to go down. The deck faced the west so they could enjoy the sunset.

Nolan took a bite of the potatoes and the garlic exploded on his tongue and the cheese was smooth and creamy. "These potatoes are awesome. Glad you decided on them instead of baked."

"Thanks, I like them too. They are faster than a baked potato from the oven and I'm not a huge fan of baked potatoes in the microwave."

Nolan grimaced. "Yeah kind of makes them all squishy."

"Exactly."

He cut off a piece of meat and chuckled. "Hey, did you hear about the fire department prank?"

"No. Tell me."

"Well you know the *bonfire* that the fire chief had in his back yard? Apparently, everyone in the vicinity of the fire has complained about mice getting in their houses. I suppose the arsonists must have burned down a mouse village. I assume the chief's house got the most mice, so it seems like just paybacks to me. But the firefighters decided to expand on the paybacks."

"They do love their pranks," Kristen said. "What did they do this time?"

"My understanding is that Terry and Kyle built a giant mouse trap and the firefighters got like a hundred large inflatable mice that they filled the yard with— some hanging off the mousetrap and some on the roof of the chief's house. I got a picture on my phone, want to see?" He brought up the picture and handed her his phone. "Although I'll be surprised if it's not in the paper tomorrow."

"Yeah, Gus loves the department pranks. The fire department summer picnic always has a couple of pages devoted to their antics. Since the police department is always invited you'll see it firsthand."

When Farley came over to beg for scraps, Kristen said to him, "No more for you dog, you've already had plenty of people-food tonight."

Nolan winced. "Saw that, did you?"

"Yes, I did." Kristen just looked at him while he fidgeted. Then she laughed, "It's okay, in moderation."

Nolan breathed a sigh of relief. "Good, he's such a well-behaved dog, I just couldn't resist."

"I know—and he looks at you with his sweet, hopeful expression."

"Right. It's all his fault for being so cute."

"Good try, Nolan, but you are the human and should, I repeat, *should*, know better."

Nolan grinned. "We all have our faults and temptations. And this household seems to be my weakness." Nolan looked at the beautiful woman across from him and felt desire for her start to spike.

She looked in his eyes and he could see passion building in her gaze too.

"So, let's carry this upstairs and see what other temptations we can indulge."

Kristen smiled. "Sounds like a plan I can get onboard with."

They got everything upstairs in one trip. Nolan loaded the dishwasher while Kristen put the food away. When she turned out of the fridge, Nolan was right there and pounced on her. He twirled her around and backed her up against the counter. Her scent was a heady combination of spicy and sweet and all her, and he was addicted. He reached up and put his hands on her face and lowered his head to kiss her.

SHE EXPECTED HIM to plunder but he surprised her and started with a soft, gentle brushing of lips. She ran her hands into his hair, the short strands tickling her fingers, and pulled his head down. He obliged her unspoken request with more pressure and more heat. She opened her mouth and his tongue swept inside to duel with hers. He tasted like garlic and sin—it was a heady combination.

She needed to touch more of him so she let her fingers slide down his back as she pulled him in tighter, closer to her body, and he didn't argue. She was wedged between his hard muscles and the counter and it felt wonderful. He drew back and kissed her eyelids and nose. Then he left a trail of fire to her ear where he softly bit the lobe, making her moan with pleasure. He kissed his way down her neck to her shoulder and nipped the soft spot where they joined. His hand had moved down to her waist holding her tight to him.

She squirmed against him making him shudder. She said, "Let's take this to the bedroom and lose the clothes."

He laughed and scooped her up over his shoulder and carried her toward the bedroom at a fast pace.

Kristen laughed as he dumped her on the bed. "Not what I was expecting, but it was very efficient. Now, lose the clothes, buster."

"Yes, ma'am."

She just watched while he shucked off his clothes, admiring the play of muscles as he moved. When he was naked he looked at her, still propped up on the bed watching.

Nolan said, "Hey, you're supposed to be getting naked too."

"Too busy watching the display. Very nice."

"Aw, shucks, ma'am," he said with false modesty. Then he pounced on her again and started *helping* her remove her clothes.

She just laughed and let him have his way. When they were both naked, he suited up, crawled onto the bed with her, and drew her close to him in a warm embrace. She reveled in the skin-on-skin feel, his hot, hard body against her.

He ran his hands down her back and squeezed her ass. "*Mmm.* Nice. I do love the feel of you next to me sweetheart. So soft."

Kristen rubbed her palms up his strong, muscular chest. Her fingers played over the ridges. His muscles twitched as she touched each one and she delighted in the power she had over this strong man. "Make love to me, Nolan."

"Oh, Kristen, I'd love to." He kissed her slowly, gently, with ever-growing passion while his firm touch ran over her body. Caressing, squeezing, teasing her responses higher and higher. He rolled her onto her back and he moved on top of her and then into her, slowly—oh, so slowly.

Kristen was out of her mind from the sensations and she moaned his name. He continued to move slowly in and out, in and out. The tension inside her built with each smooth thrust. She tilted her hips so he went deeper, touching her womb, driving her higher and higher.

He thrust faster and stronger and whispered, "Come for me, Kristen."

She whispered back, "Come *with* me." And they shattered together—spinning higher, showering the earth with sparks and light. They drifted back to themselves and she felt him pressing her into the mattress and it was glorious. The feel of his heavy body on top of her own was magnificent.

He started to move off her and she said, "Wait, just a few moments."

"I don't want to squish you."

"Just a few more moments, it feels so good."

He waited a couple of minutes and then rolled them both so she was on top. He drew the sheet up over them, so she wouldn't get chilled by the soft breeze bringing the cool air from the hills down into the valley.

"Can you stay tonight?"

"I can, but I need to leave early in the morning to get changed and ready for work."

"That's okay, as long as you put the coffee on when you leave."

He chuckled. "I can do that. I'll even let Farley out."

"Oh, bonus points for you."

"I like bonus points. Maybe I'll use them now."

"Don't you need to sleep?" She asked.

"We can sleep later."

And they did sleep later—much later.

Chapter Sixteen

THE DAY OF THE GRAND opening Kristen and Mary Ann were as ready as they could get.

Once the word was out that the gallery would be opening, a few more timid artists had come around asking if they could have their things in the gallery. One man, Cliff, who had gone to high school with Kristen brought in oil paintings of Lake Chelan and the surrounding area that were beautiful.

Another woman, Iris, brought in candles and soaps she made from local wild flowers—she sent most of her stock to galleries and gift shops in other towns. She'd never sold anything in Chedwick.

Mary Ann was incensed. "Iris, I have been taking the ferry up to Stehekin for five years to buy this soap and you make it here in town? Are you kidding me? I ration myself using it, so I don't run out before my annual trip."

Iris smiled shyly. "I'm glad you like them, Mary Ann."

"But—"

Kristen interrupted. "Thank you for bringing them in, Iris. Your soaps and candles are exquisite and we are thrilled to put them in the gallery."

Stephanie—who was a partner with Kristen's sister, Barbara—brought in quilts. She said they were a hobby and she'd never sold any but she thought she'd ask Kristen if they were good enough to put in the gallery. Of course, they were—so in the gallery they went.

Alyssa Jefferson had dragged her best friend Rachel Reardon into the gallery. "Mary Ann, you just have to see Rachel's photography."

Rachel had a small portfolio clutched to her chest. "Alyssa, no. I never would have brought this out of the house if I had known you were bringing me here. You said you wanted to look at them. They're not good enough for the gallery."

Mary Ann gently pried the portfolio away from Rachel. "Now, Rachel, let me be the judge of that."

"But—"

Alyssa interrupted. "Rachel, let Mary Ann look. Your photography is amazing."

Mary Ann opened the portfolio and gasped. Most of the pictures were 8x10 or smaller, but would look very lovely in larger sizes. She had close-ups in full color and black and white of birds and butterflies and flowers and even elk and one bear. They were matted and as Mary Ann flipped through them she was thrilled with the attention to detail and the beauty of the pictures.

"Oh, Rachel, they are certainly good enough for the gallery—in fact they should be blown up into larger sizes and be in much more important galleries than ours. These are amazing."

Rachel turned bright red. "Really? You really think so, Mary Ann?"

"I do. Let me call Kristen to come look."

Kristen came in and looked through the photographs, her eyes got wider with each piece. "Oh yeah, we are putting these near Lucille's art—they will attract the same buyers I think. Rachel, we need to get the negatives to Chelan to get some larger sizes printed and framed."

By the day of the grand opening the gallery was full and edging toward crowded. But it all looked beautiful. Samantha had made some cookies just for their opening— miniature versions of different pieces of art in the gallery. Mary Ann and Kristen planned to be there from open to close with Tammy coming in for the opening shift and Tim coming in for the closing shift. Several of the artists planned to be in attendance for questions and to lend a helping hand, if needed.

Mary Ann was planning to be the cashier and they had a small metal box they planned to use for cash or local checks. The rest of them floated to answer questions or put up sold signs on items that couldn't be carried out and would need either packaging or mailing.

Of course, they didn't know if they would have five

people come to the opening or a hundred. They had advertised, but they had no idea if that would be effective.

They opened the gallery at eleven and only Mayor Carol and Gus were there. The express ferry should have landed about ten, so they felt some disenchantment that they didn't have anyone on that shuttle, but hoped for some people on the slow ferry which would land about eleven fifteen. When noon passed, and only a few local people had stopped by, Mary Ann and Kristen were feeling very let down. All their hard work, and no one was coming into the gallery.

Kristen couldn't believe how disappointed she felt. She hadn't realized she'd gotten excited about the idea. She didn't even like talking to people and here she was heartbroken no one was coming to the gallery. She went to the back to get away from the looks of pity she was seeing.

As she stomped toward her studio she gave in to her dark thoughts. *Well, fuck this. I'll just go back up on my mountain and do my own thing. To hell with the gallery. I don't need this stress. I don't need to run a store in town. I don't need people. How did I get roped into this shit in the first place, anyway?*

She turned her head to frown at the empty gallery and there standing in the front yard was the town peacock in full array. She marched toward him. "Oh, no, you don't. You are not going to stand there looking all regal like you're putting your stamp of approval on this cluster fuck." She shook her finger at him. "This time you are dead wrong. No one is here and all these artists are going to be disappointed and it's all my fault. So you just go on and preen somewhere else." She waved her hand at him.

The peacock turned his back on her and his feathers seemed to get even bigger and fuller.

She put her hands on her hips. "Fine, be stubborn. But you're going to look like an idiot out here in front of this disaster." She stamped off toward her studio, fuming. *Stupid peacock and stupid me for talking to the stupid peacock, stupid gallery, stupid people who didn't come, stupid town, stupid life.*

Nolan found her a few minutes later. "Kristen."

"I don't want to hear it Nolan, I'm just going back up on the mountain and to hell with this damn gallery anyway. Why should people want to come here to this stupid town to see my stupid gallery anyway?"

"Oh, baby, don't say that. I came to tell you—"

"I don't want to hear it Nolan. I'm just pissed that it's a failure—a lot of people were counting on it to help their livelihood. And now— now I've failed them," she said as her eyes filled.

"But you haven't, honey. You haven't failed them."

"There sure as hell isn't anyone here—not tourists or any locals either."

"There will be, that's what I came to tell you. There was a couple of people on the lake with some big yachts. The dumb asses were driving too fast and had indulged in Bloody Mary's and Mimosas for breakfast and crashed into each other. The express ferry saw the whole thing and radioed for help. Both ferries stopped to take on some of the passengers. They called in for some help with first aid and for anyone in town to stand by to help. So, all the firefighters and anyone else that can help are down at the dock."

"But I didn't hear the siren."

"No, they just toned it out and didn't ring the siren because it wasn't an immediate emergency. They just needed people to gather for assistance at the landing. Anyone who was here at eleven missed it, since you don't have a radio.

"So, you better get out there and put on your happy face, because they should have landed about five minutes ago, and all the tourists should be arriving about now," as Nolan said that the door buzzer sounded with people coming in."

"Why are you here and not helping at the landing?"

"Because there was a crowd and the chief thought I should come relate what happened. Especially since Mayor Carol was here. I told her before I came to find you."

Kristen asked, "Is any other help needed?"

"No, just keep the folks that come in occupied. They have radioed uplake that the ferries will be delayed another hour to get everything squared away before they can continue services.

"So, everyone is trapped here for at least an hour, maybe two. Now, get out there and help your customers," Nolan said as he kissed her on the forehead and pushed her out the door toward the house.

Kristen walked back into the gallery—literally

swarming with people—and wondered if the rest of the shops in town were as crowded. She saw Nolan leave, probably to go back to help or just to keep an eye on all the stranded people.

Kristen decided to go over to her own work first, since she knew the most about it. She did hear a number of positive comments, as she wove her way through the crowd. Several other artists had also gathered since the crisis was under control.

When she got over to her jewelry there were many people looking into the different displays she'd put her work in. She walked back behind the counter where she could open the showcases if anyone asked.

"It's about time you showed up to let us see this jewelry. It seems like we've been standing here waiting for help forever," said a particularly cranky looking man.

His wife said, "Now honey we've only been in the building two minutes. You can go wait outside, if you would rather."

"And leave you in here alone with the credit card? I think not."

The woman just rolled her eyes at Kristen and asked to see one of the smaller necklaces. Kristen got the piece out and handed it to the woman.

"Well, that *is* kind of pretty," the man said. "Do you want it?"

"I like it very much."

There were two women who looked to be in their mid-twenties looking at some earrings. One of them asked

Kristen, "Can we look at those earrings? Do you have more than one set that would be matching?"

"Each earring is hand made so they aren't exactly alike, but I do have several pairs in the same pattern."

"Goody! Can we look at several of them?"

Kristen got the little tray with the multiple sets out from the storage cabinet below and placed it on the counter.

Then she turned back to the grumpy couple who looked at Kristen and the man asked, "Are these firm prices, or are they negotiable?"

"They are firm. It's what I sell them for in other galleries in the state. Although we are giving a ten percent discount, today only, for our opening day."

"That's something at least." Then he turned to his wife and said, "If you get the necklace then that's all for the remainder of the trip."

"Yes, dear." Looking at Kristen the woman asked, "So, are you the jewelry designer?"

"Yes, I am," Kristen said.

The man said, "Then you can set whatever price you like."

"I can, but this is the price I charge for this necklace. I can raise it another fifty dollars if you really want to pay more, but this is the lowest it's going to go."

The man sputtered. "Well, I nev—"

His wife interrupted. "We'll take it. Where do we pay?"

Kristen told them and heaved a sigh of relief as the couple walked off, still bickering.

The two ladies had decided on a pair of earrings

each and Kristen put the rest back in the bottom of the display case. Kristen knew it might be a long time before the women got to the front to pay. She kept up a steady stream of customers and as people selected their treasures, she kept a running list of what was purchased.

After what seemed like days rather than a few hours, she heard the ferry horn honk, signaling it was getting ready to leave. She raised her voice and yelled above the crowd. "The ferry is getting ready to leave. Please settle up, if you intend to be on it."

She locked her jewelry case and walked toward the front asking people as she went if she could help them. Some of the other artists noticed what she was doing and started mimicking her, so they were all effectively herding the people toward the door. Kristen saw that Mary Ann was overwhelmed with the number of people purchasing items so she and Tim started helping her cash out the remaining people. Tim did credit card purchases while Mary Ann handled the cash sales and Kristen worked with the people who needed their items shipped. Some of the artists helped wrap fragile items and put them into bags or boxes.

The ferry blasted its horn one more time and Kristen knew that was the ten-minute warning. So, leaving Greg and Terry who had shown up about a half hour earlier taking down shipping information, she did one last sweep through the store.

She noticed one young man, who looked a little ragged, off to the side watching Mary Ann closely as she took the cash payments. Kristen walked over to him to ask if he needed help with something.

He looked a little startled and then in a rush said, "No, gotta go. Bye." And he nearly ran out the door and down the street. When he went the opposite direction from where the ferry was, she tried to call out to him—to tell him he was going the wrong way—but he just ran faster down the street away from the landing.

Kristen shook her head and went back into the gallery where the last two people were finishing up their transactions. When they were out the door, Kristen and several others collapsed to the floor with a groan.

"Well, that was crazy," Terry said.

Mary Ann just laughed at him. "You only saw the last bit, Terry. It was completely packed in here and people must have asked a thousand questions. And then they bought everything in sight."

Tim whistled. "The total on the credit card machine is half a mil."

Kristen sat up from where she had been laying on the dirty floor, too exhausted to move. "What? A half a million dollars?"

"Yep we sold a couple of Lucille's art and a shit ton of everything else."

Mary Ann reached into the little tin box and brought out handfuls of money. "Oh, yeah. We had a very successful first day."

"Of course, there had to be a disaster to cause it."

Greg said, "No, I don't think so. When we were helping

at the landing, I heard a lot of people say they were coming solely to see our gallery."

"I think that's true, Greg, because I asked a bunch of them if they were only here because they were stranded in Chedwick and they said no—they were on the ferry for the grand opening."

Terry scratched his head. "I don't think anyone was stranded here."

"But Nolan said—"

Terry interrupted. "Oh, that's why you're confused. We sent Nolan to let you know what was going on, before they decided to send the express ferry uplake with everyone who was going uplake and then use the big ferry to take everyone back. Although I know the express is going to stop back by to make sure everyone who wanted to go back to Chelan got a ride that direction."

"So, everyone who came into the gallery was on their way here? Not just stranded?" Kristen asked.

"Correct," Terry said as Mayor Carol walked into the gallery.

"Oh, my. I had no idea the turnout would be so large."

Mayor Carol said, "Kristen, the ferry people told me that they had to turn people away today because they were at capacity and they asked if you would please extend the grand opening through the weekend."

"Of course. I should have thought of that to begin with."

"Good. I assured them you would, because they had

to tell the people they turned away this morning that you would, so they didn't have a riot on their hands."

"Seriously?"

"Yes, dear," Mayor Carol answered.

"I'm not sure we have enough stock for two more days like this one," Kristen said with a note of panic in her voice.

"I suggest that everyone who is here go home and bring whatever else they have that can be sold, and that you call all the rest of the artists, and tell them you need more of everything. In fact, lets divvy up the phone calls among us here, so we can get everyone called quickly. Because you'll need time to get it priced and out on display."

"Great idea Mayor Carol." She looked at Mary Ann. "You keep the place open, in the event there are any locals or people staying overnight that come in, since we're technically open a few more hours. While the rest of us go to gather more stock, okay?"

"Will do."

Everyone agreed to that idea and they scattered to make their calls and gather up more goods to sell.

Chapter Seventeen

THEY ENDED UP WORKING late that night receiving and setting up the new stock. Nolan came by after his shift and brought pizza for everyone that was helping, guessing everyone would be starving. Kristen said she was so damn grateful for that, she could have kissed him. In fact, once they got everyone out of the gallery, she did just that.

"Thank you for bringing food and helping tonight. Dear God, I had no idea this was going to be so crazy. I hope it won't always be this busy, because I don't have enough staff for that."

Nolan rubbed his thumb across her knuckles. "It won't be. Right now it's new and exciting and everyone wants to see it. Plus, it's still tourist season so there are a lot of people on the lake and in the neighboring towns."

"Good."

"Although, I did call my mom and asked her to send more of her work, just in case. And I think it might be wise to hire a few more people."

Kristen whined. "Can we just go to bed now, I'm too tired to think of anything else."

"Oh, am I staying for bed?" Nolan teased.

"Hell yes! I need some reward for all that hard work and dealing with all those people."

He laughed. "And I'm your reward?"

"Yes, you are. I need to let Farley out."

"Okay I'll gather up the pizza trash, lock up down here, and meet you upstairs."

"My hero."

As Nolan did as promised he found a window open over on the far wall. It was a little difficult to shut, but he muscled it down and locked it. He put the trash by the back door—to put out the next morning—and went upstairs to be a reward. Not a bad job, being the prize, in fact, he decided he liked that idea. He might just like being her payment for a long time. Forever? He didn't know about that. Maybe he'd need to think about that a bit more.

KRISTEN WAS STILL overwhelmed by what had happened that day and couldn't imagine many more days like today.

She decided she'd think about that later. Right now, she had a yummy man waiting for her and he'd help relieve the stress she could feel in her neck and shoulders. Her and Farley went up the outside stairs. Farley saw Nolan and made a beeline for him—it looked like Nolan was now one of Farley's favorite people. Nolan crouched down and gave the happy dog a full body rub.

Farley licked Nolan, who laughed. "I think it's the pizza smell from me cleaning up."

Kristen shook her head. "Maybe some of it, but I think he just likes you. I know how he feels."

"Do you now? Let me get washed up and I can give you a full body rub, without the pizza smell."

Kristen laughed. "Best offer I've had all day. Did you bring the money box up?"

Nolan walked over to the kitchen sink and started washing, "Yes. When did you say the safe was coming?"

"Wednesday. And the alarm people are coming Thursday, so I should be fully secure by Friday."

"You should probably make deposits each night until then. Tonight, we can take a pass, since you have your very own personal police officer guarding you and the money. I can drop it by the bank in the morning."

Kristen laughed at his puffed-out chest. "I thought about that tonight, but then I wasn't sure how much cash to keep, for starting money tomorrow, and I was just too tired to reason it out."

"I know—I was pretty surprised at the number of people who came today. And the ferry company said they have already sold out most of the trips for the weekend."

"Okay enough talk about scary stuff. Let's make out," Kristen said.

"You've got it." Nolan pulled her into his arms and gave her a warm, wet kiss.

Kristen pressed up against him and put her head on his shoulder. She did feel safe in his embrace. She ran her hands up his back to his shoulders as he pulled her tighter against him. It was amazing how well they fit together. Like two puzzle pieces. She loved the way her body felt against his; she just wanted to melt into him.

"*Mmm.* You feel so good," he said.

"I was thinking the same thing."

"Great minds and all that," Nolan said.

"So, do you want to go snuggle on the couch or go straight to bed?"

Nolan frowned. "Those are both great options. I'm off tomorrow, so I was thinking I could help in the gallery, if you want an extra pair of hands. The point of that statement is that I don't have to get up early, so we've got lots of time."

"Oh, having you around to help would be great. It was so frantic today."

"I don't think it will be quite as bad tomorrow, because you won't be getting both ferries at the same time."

"Oh, true. Well, that might help a lot, but a few extra hands won't hurt anyway. Let's go snuggle on the couch for a while—we can put on a movie or watch some TV. I almost never do that."

"Perfect."

THEY PICKED OUT a light comedy and snuggled on the couch. About three quarters of the way through the movie Nolan felt her body soften as she drifted off to sleep. He wasn't terribly surprised given the stressful day it had been. He wasn't disappointed either—he'd carry her to bed and let her rest. She'd put on yoga pants and a T-shirt earlier, so she could stay in those without being uncomfortable. He could hold her while she slept, and that sounded just fine to him.

KRISTEN WOKE UP very warm. She was in her bed, still dressed, with a hot man wrapped around her. But it was clearly morning, so she wondered how she'd gotten there. She didn't remember going to sleep—in fact the last thing she could recall was watching a movie with Nolan. She must have fallen asleep during the movie and the poor man must have carried her down the hall and put her to bed. Damn, and she'd missed all the fun they could have had all night. Not that it was too late for horizontal sports. Since it was early, and the gallery wouldn't open until eleven, they had plenty of time to enjoy each other.

But first, she needed to heed the call of nature—then she would come back and take advantage of the sleepy man under her covers.

She started to slip out of bed but he held on tighter. She whispered, "Got to pee, be right back."

He mumbled incoherently but let her go. She used the bathroom and brushed her teeth and left her clothes hanging on the back of the door. When she got back in bed he automatically closed his arms around her. Almost immediately his hands started wandering over her naked body and she could feel him begin to wake up. She let her hands move, caressing him too. He'd only worn his briefs to bed, so there was plenty of warm skin to feel.

"*Mmm*. Naked," he muttered. "Like it."

"I thought you might. It didn't take you long to notice, even asleep," she said kissing his nose.

"Felt different. Had to find out why," he said with his eyes still closed, his hands still moving.

"I thought it might be fun to wake you up with a little skin-on-skin."

"Fun, uh huh, fun."

"You obviously carried me to bed last night and tucked me in, so that deserves a reward for being a gentleman and letting me sleep."

"Felt nice to hold you sleeping," he said, still relaxed with his eyes closed. "Feels even better now."

"Does it?" she said running her hand down his chest to find him fully aroused. Taking him in her hand, she stroked up and down a couple of times. "It does seem like there is a part of you fully awake."

"Yes," he said, finally opening his eyes and smiling at her. "And now you've woken the rest of me and must pay the fee."

"Oh, and what is the fee?"

"This," he said as his mouth came down on hers and he pulled her in tight against his hard body, half-covering her as he pulled her close to him. "You taste minty—I should go brush, too."

"Oh no, you don't. Do not stop what you're doing. I have enough minty for both of us."

"As you wish," he said as his mouth returned to hers with a vengeance. One hand went up into her hair and the other cupped her breast bringing the nipple to a tight bud. "You are so beautiful."

"It's still dark—you can't see me."

He huffed. "Pretty literal for this early in the morning."

"Just keeping it real."

"Fine, but I have seen you naked in the light and I know these nipples are a dusky rose color offset against your petal pink skin, until you get to where the sun has kissed you from being outdoors. And then down here,"— he said as his hands roamed down her torso— "we have your pretty—"

"Okay, I give up. That's a little too literal."

"But I was just getting to the good part," Nolan grumbled.

"I think we can find better things for your mouth to do than describe my every asset."

"Good idea. Yes, we can," he said as he slid under the covers and nipped her belly and hip and then parted her legs to put his mouth at ground zero.

Kristen moaned as he parted her folds and tasted.

"*Mmm*. Ambrosia," he said.

The vibration sent awareness winging through her, igniting nerve endings from her toes to the top of her head and back again. And then he feasted and she hung on for dear life to the sheets.

He was relentless, licking, tasting, nibbling, sucking. He drove her higher and higher, sensation upon sensation. She felt her body stiffen and he slid two fingers in her and rubbed on the inside as he sucked hard on her clit.

A huge wave of release hit her hard and she moaned, and then another wave hit—again and again, each wave more intense than the last until she screamed. He gentled his touch as every last bit of her emptied. Then he moved up her body, held her and gently stroked her as she came down from the most intense orgasm she'd ever felt. And if truth be told, had never truly believed even existed. She knew better now—dear God, did she know better.

Through the haze in her mind she vaguely heard Nolan tell Farley to hush. When she was finally coherent and could speak, she asked, "What was that?"

"Just putting my mouth to good use, as instructed."

"I think you killed me. My throat is even sore."

He kissed her cheek, "You did scream a bit, I had to tell

Farley to be quiet, and it's a good thing you're in a business district, or we would be answering the door to the police about now."

She could still hear Farley whining next to the door. "It's okay Farley go lay down now." She called out to her dog and then turned towards her man. "Yes, that is a good thing—because there is something very hard poking into my side, that I think we need to take care of, and it wouldn't be fun to be interrupted."

He laughed. "No, it would be rather embarrassing to have the police show up at the door to see if I was murdering you. Embarrassing for weeks, in fact. So, you're ready to commence with the *fun?*"

"Yes sir. Suit up and let's have more *fun.*"

He reached into her nightstand and retrieved a foil packet and tore it open with his teeth.

Kristen took the condom from him. "Here, let me help."

She enjoyed watching Nolan's eyes glaze over as she gave him pleasure, while she protected them both. He said, "You have to stop that or we'll have to wait a while for more *fun.*"

"Spoil sport."

"Not at all, just trying to have more *fun* as you requested, my dear," he said as he slid inside her—deep inside her.

"*Mmm.* Okay, you win, that feels nice."

"Nice, huh? Well, let's see if we can up that estimation, shall we?" he said as he started moving.

She wrapped her legs around his waist and he slid in deeper. "Oh yeah, that's good."

"Let me know when we hit awesome or stupendous, even."

"Will do. Feeling better all the time."

He put his mouth on her right nipple and drew it into his mouth suckling the tight bud and scraping it with his teeth, as he pulled his mouth off and moved to the other breast. Kristen moaned at the sensations he was causing and grabbed his ass to hold on as he spun her higher. He kissed his way up her neck and nipped at the soft spot between the neck and shoulder and then kept moving up to her ear, where he pulled her earlobe into his mouth and bit down lightly.

"Oh my God," she said as her body started to tighten.

He let go of her earlobe and ravaged her mouth, his tongue mimicking the in and out of his penis. "Come now," he commanded. And she did. Hard. Her inner muscles milked him and he came right along with her, with a shout.

He collapsed on her and she held him tight and whispered, "Awesome, stupendous, amazing, marvelous."

He laughed and rolled them so she was on top.

She pulled the sheet up over their cooling bodies and as she drifted to sleep said, "Incredible, Fantastic."

Chapter Eighteen

A FEW HOURS LATER, FARLEY started whining to be let out so Nolan got up and found his pants and slipped them on commando—he didn't want to have to look for his shorts. It was warm out even at nine in the morning, so he'd be fine barefooted and with no shirt.

Kristen sat up. "I'll make coffee while you let him out."

When Nolan got back from letting the dog out Kristen was in the kitchen in his T-shirt and possibly nothing else. He walked up behind her and wrapped his arms around her. "You look good in my shirt—better than I look." She wiggled her butt back against him. *Oh, yeah. Nothing else for sure.*

"You better stop that or your coffee is going to get cold."

"No time for that now, we have to get dressed and

ready for a new day in the gallery," she said as she wiggled against him, again.

He took his coffee cup, stepped back, and gave her a light swat on the ass. "Bad girl."

"That's not what you said earlier."

He swatted her one more time. "Yeah, but that's when we had time to follow through on your enticing behavior."

Kristen laughed as she turned around to face him. She looked down and ran her hand over the front of his jeans. "Poor baby, not enough action for you this morning?"

He grabbed her hand and kissed it. "Never enough where you're concerned."

She grinned. "Good to know. Want some breakfast? I have eggs I can scramble."

"Sure. You make the eggs, I'll make the toast."

"Deal." Kristen kissed him on the lips as she passed by him to get to the fridge, where she took out eggs, cheese, spinach, a couple slices of ham, and one sweet red pepper. She handed Nolan butter and orange juice. She cut up the ham and chopped the peppers and put it in with the eggs to start cooking. She added the spinach when the eggs were nearly done so it wasn't too soggy, and threw the cheese in at the last minute. She slid one portion onto each plate as Nolan finished buttering the last piece of toast. He'd poured them nice glasses of orange juice and had found some blackberry jam to use if they wanted.

Nolan sat at the table. "This is quite a feast."

"I figured we needed good fuel to get us through the day."

Nolan nodded. "Maybe we should get Amber to send us over something to eat—about one—that we can eat in shifts. You know—something that will keep, without going bad."

"Good idea. I'll give her a call and set something up. I think everyone was starving yesterday by the time we got the pizza. Better not to kill our friends by starvation."

When they finished eating, Nolan pushed his plate away. "That was delicious. Thanks for making it."

"You're welcome—and now I think we better get dressed, so that when the team gets here we aren't sitting here half naked. Of course, that would be better than sitting here half naked when the tourists, aliens, and monsters arrive."

Nolan laughed. "Aliens and monsters?"

"Kristen shrugged. "Tourists, aliens, monsters. Same, same."

"You are terrible."

"I know, but that's why you love me."

"Yes, I do." And at that statement they both got quiet, after realizing what they had both said. Then Nolan took her hand. "You know I said that flippantly, but I really do think it might be true."

Kristen sighed. "Yeah, I think it *might be true* back at you."

He grinned. "Awesome. Well, beautiful, let's go have a shower and maybe celebrate a little of that *might be true* stuff."

They put their breakfast dishes into the dishwasher and

headed off to the bathroom with her head on his shoulder and his arm wrapped around her waist. They got into the shower and while the steam rose, so did their passion. As the hot water poured over them, he kissed her with a fire that made the liquid seem cool. And they made love with a focus and intensity that their previous encounters had lacked. In the shower, she felt like they became one, giving and receiving love and joy and a trust she had never known before. When the water started turning cold, she sighed and got out of the shower to dry off and return to the real world. But she kept that interlude hidden in her heart, away from the cares and reality of life, in a special place where she could retrieve it whenever she needed to. And she felt changed and wondered if he felt the same.

NOLAN WAS ABOUT TO open the door when Mary Ann walked in. "I took the trash out, after I cleaned up a horrible mess from the bears last night. It looked like there had been a war in the trash. It took me a while to get it all cleaned up, I didn't know bears made such a mess."

"I don't know much about bears and their habits either. I'm sorry you had a mess to clean up, you beat me to it by just a few minutes. I was just about to take the trash and let the mutt here out," he said gesturing at Farley who was happily trying to snag Mary Ann's attention for a pat or a snack. He didn't seem to be discriminating in his choice of affection.

Mary Ann laughed and gave him a good scratching behind his ears and then opened the door to let him out. "I came a little early to get ready for the hordes."

Nolan laughed. "Kristen called them aliens and monsters."

"Not surprising—she's not exactly the most outgoing person on the planet."

"Hey, I heard that," Kristen said coming into the room. "And I agree with every word. So, does that mean I get a pass and can go hide, ahem, work in my studio rather than face the hordes?"

"Absolutely not," Mary Ann said.

Nolan shook his head. "Nope, you're going to be right here with the rest of us."

"Damn," Kristen muttered. "Then I suppose we better get after it. We've got about an hour and a half before the ferry and I expect some of our other *worker slash volunteers* will be showing up any time now, so we better get the front door open. I talked to Amber and she's going to bring by some food to keep us going through the day. And she said Samantha was up half the night baking more cookies, to keep us stocked for the aliens—I mean, tourists."

THE SECOND DAY of the gallery opening looked to be just as fruitful, but with more help and better planning it wasn't nearly as exhausting. The ferries coming in at their regularly scheduled time made a big difference, too, by spreading out the people arriving over a longer period. The staggered landings and departures made a more even flow, so they could get people serviced in a much better fashion.

Kristen ended up near her jewelry all morning. With people asking her about custom pieces and questions about how she worked, it was nearly enjoyable. Not that she would ever admit that. To anyone. Ever.

The worst part of the whole day was that Nolan was clear over on the other side of the gallery by his mother's work, answering questions and telling people about the glass design industry. It would have been more fun to have him closer. His revelation this morning had pretty much made her day. Week. Month. Maybe even year. Yes, she was falling in love with him—that was becoming obvious. She didn't really know what to do with that, since she'd never been in love before. What would happen when she went back up the mountain after the forest fires were out? Did she want to go back up? Living here in town hadn't been too awful and she did love the studio. But what about her solitude and privacy on the mountain? Would she miss it? She had no idea.

"Excuse me, miss?" said a tourist.

Shaking herself back to the present, she smiled. "What can I help you with?"

NOLAN COULDN'T BELIEVE he was actually enjoying talking about glass design. He really had thought that part of his life was gone forever. He didn't often think of doing glasswork, but talking to the tourists about his mother's art had made it clear to him that he missed it. He realized he wanted to make something for Kristen—she inspired and stirred the creativity within him.

He'd had other girlfriends before but none that moved him like she did. She was so beautiful and caring and he was flat crazy about her. He knew he was falling in love and that kind of scared the crap out of him. What did he know about being in love? He'd closed off his heart when his sister had been murdered and he'd never intended to change that. But Kristen had just moved right in without him even noticing and now she was firmly established there. He wasn't a hundred percent sure he even liked the idea, but there wasn't much he could do about it now.

And if she moved back up the mountain when the forest fire was over? He would just drive on up there. Maybe not every night, but enough of them. Maybe she'd drive down some nights. He wondered if she'd consider staying here in town—in this place, or his. It was too early to think about all that, since the forest fires would probably not be completely out for another couple of months—until they got the first decent snow.

Kristen decided to take her lunch break as the people taking the express ferry were starting to leave. She got some salad and a sandwich from the food Amber had brought over and decided to go out and eat with Farley. Nolan was busy with a couple of customers and she had been neglecting her poor dog the last few days. She walked out and saw him sleeping in the shade, so she went closer and then called his name to wake him up, but he didn't move. She called him once more and then noticed he'd been throwing up again. She dropped her food and ran over to him to see if he was breathing. He was, but he certainly wasn't moving. She ran back into the gallery. Nolan looked at her and immediately excused himself, rushing over to her.

"What's wrong?"

"Farley. He's not moving and he's been sick again."

"Let's go look." They ran out into the yard and Nolan ran ahead of her and knelt to put his ear down to listen for a heartbeat. "He's still alive—he's breathing and his heart is beating. But I think you better get him into Chelan this time and have him examined."

Kristen nodded, but didn't move.

"Come on, sweetheart. Let's get to the dock. The express ferry will get us there the quickest. I've got a blanket in my car we can carry him in."

Kristen nodded, but still didn't move.

Nolan spoke harshly, "Kristen, snap out of it. We have to get moving. Go get your purse and meet me at the car. Now."

Kristen blinked and then took off at a run to the house. She grabbed her purse, told Mary Ann they had to get Farley to Chelan, and ran out to meet Nolan who had the dog loaded in the car.

"I called the ferry and told them we were coming. Call the vet and tell him we're on the way."

Kristen scrolled through her contacts for the vet and pushed the call button with shaking hands. She told the vet's office they were on their way and was told they would have someone meet them at the dock. They got on the ferry and the operator told them they would push it a little faster for them. There was no change in Farley—he still wasn't moving but he was breathing, so all she could do was wait.

Forty-five minutes later they were the first off the ferry at Field's Point landing. The vet had a car there and they took off quickly into Chelan.

When they arrived at the clinic the vet examined Farley, took some blood and some X-rays. Then he told her, "He's going to be okay. But I don't know what has caused this, so I want to run some tests and keep Farley at least overnight. No, two nights, since it's the weekend. I won't get the tests back until Monday."

Kristen said, "Oh, two nights, I can—"

Interrupting, the vet said, "You might as well go home, there isn't anything you can do here. I suppose you could stay in a hotel, but you still won't be able to do anything until Monday at the earliest. And I do think he'll be just fine—he's really acting like he's just asleep, no other symptoms other than his stomach seems to be rumbling and upset. But his heart is fine, the X-rays don't show anything, and everything else seems okay, too. I've taken some blood tests and that's about all we can do until Monday—other than monitor his condition and make sure he doesn't worsen."

Kristen slumped. "All right, but can you keep me informed?"

"Yes I will." Looking at Nolan he said, "I assume you can pull some strings and get you both home tonight, officer?"

Nolan nodded. "Since I'm scheduled to work tomorrow morning, that's a given."

"Good. Now, Kristen, I have your number, so after I check on him in the morning I'll give you a call."

She nodded and Nolan took her hand. "Come on, sweetheart, let's go home."

"I'll be back on the Express on Monday then," she said to the vet and they left the building.

Nolan said there was a boat waiting at the Chelan landing for them to take back. It was only a few blocks away so they walked that direction. He asked, "Do you want to get something to take with us to eat?"

Kristen nodded. "I'm kind of hungry."

So, while Nolan got them some sandwiches from the deli, she called Mary Ann to let her know they were on their way back.

"How's Farley?" Mary Ann said as she answered the phone.

"The vet said he should be fine, but they are going to keep him a few days to run some tests. We're coming back—Nolan got a private boat to bring us back tonight."

"Oh good. I was worried about Farley—and you, for that matter."

"We'll both be fine. I probably won't be there for another hour or so."

"No worries. Most of the customers are gone, so I'll close up the gallery tonight. What do you want me to do with the money?"

"Can you do a night drop on your way home? Leave a couple hundred for startup cash tomorrow and deposit the rest."

"Okay, I'll put it in the workroom."

"Good, see you tomorrow."

Chapter Nineteen

Kristen was so glad to be back home. What a horrendous end to a day that was. Her poor dog—she hoped the vet could figure out what was wrong with him. She just wanted to go to bed and sleep for a week or two; she was totally drained. When Nolan had asked if she wanted him to stay, she'd encouraged him to go to his house. She just didn't have the energy to deal with him. He needed to work in the morning, so he'd need a clean uniform and would have to get up early. Nolan reluctantly agreed that it might be easier. And when she told him she was going straight to bed, he'd agreed she probably needed the rest because of the trauma.

And that's exactly what she did. She didn't go through the gallery. She didn't check to see if it was all locked up. She didn't turn on lights in her living space. She went up the outside stairs, locked the door, dropped her purse on the table, stripped her clothes off on her way to her room, and fell flat on her face in bed. She just barely managed to get the covers over herself before she was asleep.

NOLAN DROVE BACK to his house wondering about Farley's sudden sickness. Kristen and the vet both said this was highly unusual for the dog. He'd always been a healthy animal with no health problems. She'd looked so bereft when the vet said he needed to keep Farley for two nights. He hadn't really wanted to leave her alone, but she insisted and she did look exhausted. He hoped she really would go to bed and sleep.

On the other hand, Nolan had been itching all day for some drawing paper. He had an idea for glass Kristen had inspired and he wanted to get it down on paper. Whether he'd actually create it he didn't know, but he needed to get it drawn up. He knew he had a sketchbook and colored pencils in the house. He'd never gotten away from the habit of having them near, even if he didn't use them. He'd started drawing at a very young age and he felt naked, or something, without paper and pen handy. He'd even bought some of the new advanced watercolor colored pencils because he just couldn't resist. He was going to be trying them out tonight.

Nolan finally stopped at two in the morning. He'd

drawn the glass sculpture over and over until he finally had it just right. He had a half a dozen final sketches of it from different angles. It was beautiful. Could he actually create it—he wanted to, his fingers itched to. His mind whirled with the process and how he'd accomplish it. Each step was crystal clear in his mind. It would take him several weeks, maybe even a month or more, with his other commitments. But could he do it? He didn't know, but his equipment had arrived, so he put the drawings aside and set up his gear. It would take some time to get the kiln and glory hole up to temp to melt the glass. The idea both thrilled him and made him nauseous.

He'd have to cross that bridge later, because now he needed to sleep. He was on duty in a few hours.

Kristen woke with a start at two in the morning. She listened carefully to see what might have startled her, but she didn't hear anything. Her bladder decided to make itself known, so she padded to the bathroom. She had on a tank bra and panties since she'd been too damn exhausted to even put on a T-shirt. She flushed and started back to bed, when she heard a soft bang. Was that in the house? No, probably just those damn bears or raccoons. There was pizza trash out there. And she'd just dropped her sandwich in the yard so that would certainly attract them. She sighed, grabbed a T-shirt to put on, and went back to bed—she'd deal with bears and trash mess in the morning. She hoped her poor dog was okay—maybe he'd gotten into some trash, too. Maybe she should look for some trash cans that were more bear-proof.

She nestled into the side of the bed Nolan had slept on last night and could still smell him on the pillow. She was kind of sorry, now, that she'd sent him home. His strong, warm body would have been nice to snuggle into. *Maybe I can convince him to come over tonight*—and with that thought, she drifted off to sleep.

She woke up a few hours later, took a shower and got dressed. She needed caffeine. Too bad she'd been too groggy to think about that before she showered. Damn, it would be all hot and ready if she'd had her head on straight.

She put grounds in the pot, poured the water in, set it to brew and put some bread in the toaster. She could make some eggs or something, but that seemed like a lot of work and she didn't feel up to it. Toast would have to work—at least for a little while. She poured herself a cup as soon as there was enough in the pot to fill a mug. She smiled thinking of Nolan's fancy coffee and real cream. She was good with anything that turned the water black—hot and black with maybe a crumb of sugar if she was feeling like sweetness. Usually she liked it straight out of the pot—the stronger the better. She took the first big drink and felt the warmth and the caffeine hit her system. Yay.

She took her toast and ate a couple of bites, but she really just wanted the caffeine so she put the toast down and took up her mug when she heard some god-awful caterwauling coming from the gallery. She jerked and some of the java splashed onto her hand. She swore, put the mug down on the counter and marched over to the door while wiping the wetness on her jeans.

She heard Mary Ann screeching at the top of her lungs and opened the door expecting to see blood and mayhem.

"Mary Ann, what's wrong?"

"Oh, thank heavens, you're all right."

"Of course I'm all right. What...."

Mary Ann said into her phone, "Yes ma'am, a burglary I think. The back door was wide open and a window, too." She listened, "Yes, in the gallery. No, I didn't touch anything. Yes, she seems to be fine. Yes, we'll go lock ourselves into the living quarters right now." Mary Ann raced up the stairs and dragged her into the room, then she slammed the door shut and locked it with both the handle lock and the deadbolt and then she pulled Kristen to the back, to make sure it was secured too.

"Mary Ann what in the fuck is going on?"

Mary Ann sat down hard at the kitchen table. "I think we've been robbed or burglarized or...."

"What?" she said heading toward the stairs into the gallery.

Mary Ann grabbed her arm, hauled her back, pushed her down at the table, and handed her the coffee and toast. "Drink your coffee and let me explain."

"Right. Okay, tell me what you saw."

"The trash is dumped out...."

"Oh, bears or raccoons...."

"No, now just listen. The trash is dumped out into piles. The trash barrels are in a pyramid up to that window we open for fresh air and the screen is off. And the back door was standing wide open."

Kristen heard a siren screaming toward them and tires squealing. Then she heard someone charging up the back stairs and finally Nolan yelled, "Kristen, open up!" as he pounded on the back door.

She jumped up and opened the door and he yanked her into him. "Are you okay?"

"Yes."

"Are you sure? Should I call an ambulance?"

"Nolan, stop. I'm fine. I didn't even know anything had happened until Mary Ann came screaming in the house. So, other than both of you scaring the crap out of me, I'm just fine."

He muttered, "Thank God." And dragged her into his arms nearly squeezing her to death.

She patted his back and said, "It's okay. I'm okay. Breathe, baby. It's okay, I'm not hurt."

Another car came screaming into the driveway and another pair of feet charging up the back stairs. This time, Chris yelled, "Kristen, where are you?"

"Right here, Chris, and I'm just…" she said as Chris yanked her out of Nolan's arms and into his.

Another car came screaming in and this time it was Greg. And then Kyle and then Terry and then Barbara. *Oh, for God's sake how long is this going to go on?* She finally grabbed the radio from Greg and said into it, "This is

Kristen and I'm fine. Calm the fuck down everyone."

Greg flinched. "You can't say the *F*-word on the radio."

"Too late."

NOLAN ORDERED EVERYONE but Greg to stay in the living quarters while they went down into the gallery to check things out. Officer Ben drove up as backup and even a couple of other off duty officers arrived—including the chief of police.

Nolan sent Ben up to take Mary Ann and Kristen's statements. He sent one of the off-duty officers out to keep the rest of the whole damn town from coming in and destroying the evidence. He sent the other off-duty officer to get the fingerprint kit. And then, he told Chief James Macgregor what he knew so far.

Nolan had been in a pretty big panic to make sure Kristen was safe, but he'd noticed the trash overturned and the barrels stacked in a pyramid up to that window he'd shut a couple of nights ago, and he noticed the screen had been torn off. As he talked, he saw the puzzle pieces fit together. For Pete's sake, this had been going on for days and he'd never put two and two together.

Damn it, what a fuck up he was. There were no damn bears or raccoons. Kristen wasn't putting the damn trash cans upside down—the perp was, and Farley had most likely been poisoned. He should just turn in his frickin' badge because he was clearly too much of a dumbass to have one.

But instead of saying all that, he told the chief about all the evidence and circumstances over the last two weeks in a concise manner. And then they all started looking around for confirmation and clues to the identity of the unknown subject. Ben came down to say Mary Ann had deposited most of the money last night and there was only about three hundred dollars in the metal box they used to keep the money. Nolan went into Mary Ann's workroom and, sure enough, the box was there on the floor—open and empty. They might be able to get prints from that. If they did and the unsub's prints were in the database they might be able to find out who he was. He didn't think a lot of people had handled it—Mary Ann, Kristen, and maybe one or two others. But for the most part, Mary Ann had been the money keeper.

They had no idea if anything else had been stolen. It would take some time to go over records and inventory and see if there were any discrepancies. Ben went back up to get Kristen's statement while they dusted for fingerprints on the window frame, cashbox, and backdoor handle. Then they went outside and did the same on the trashcans and window screen. They lifted a few prints, which they would have to check against the people whose prints *should* be on them.

Ben came back down with an approximate timeline based on Kristen's statement.

Ben reported, "Kristen said she was startled awake

about two in the morning, but didn't hear anything out of the ordinary, so went to the bathroom. After she flushed she heard a noise. She said it wasn't loud so she assumed it was bears or something outside."

Chief Macgregor nodded. "Unsub probably thought she was in Chelan with her dog and got scared when she flushed. Dropped the cash box and took off."

Nolan ran his hand around the back of his neck. "Probably. I encouraged her to come home, otherwise she probably would have still been in Chelan." And he'd been working on the design for the damn glass sculpture, while the woman he loved was being burglarized by some unknown subject. What was it with the glass and putting women in danger? Was it cursed or something? To hell with it—he was going to burn those damn pictures and drop his equipment into the lake.

Chief Macgregor said, "No worries—she was safe and there might have been more theft if she hadn't scared the thief off. This guy doesn't seem to be your run-of-the-mill thief. He never does any damage and he doesn't take a lot—just small things. Other than the dog being poisoned, which is different. We'll have to see what it was, once the vet gets the tests back. I wonder if the dog will be able to alert us to who it is, if he comes in contact with him. Tainting food might leave a scent he could pick up on. Something to think about, if you see the dog acting funny toward someone."

Nolan nodded. "I'll tell Kristen to keep an eye on him."

"Other than having the ladies look through the rooms,

I think we've done about all we can. I'll take the fingerprints in and get the reports started. Nolan, you stay here and find out from the women if anything else was taken and I'll pull the rest of the officers off with me. We'll need to get everyone to come in and be fingerprinted."

Nolan asked his boss, "Do you want to allow them to open today or keep it as a crime scene?"

"No need for a crime scene. Go ahead and let them reopen if they are feeling up to it. Didn't the ferry company say they had more people coming in today?"

"Yes, but there are other things in town they could do."

Chief Macgregor thought about that. "Naw, no need. They've got some time before the first ferry arrives so if they want to open, let them and if they don't, let me know and we'll redirect the passengers to other places. If we do that though it might be a pretty big hassle if people are coming strictly for the opening, but it's up to Kristen and Mary Ann. We'll do whatever they want."

"Right. If you don't hear from me, assume they are planning to open. Kristen is pretty stubborn, so I don't think this will slow her down," Nolan said with a sigh.

The chief laughed. "You've got that right." Then he turned his attention to Greg who had been a silent observer. "Thanks for giving our boy backup today, Greg. You can give Ben your statement to follow protocol, then you're free to go, or stay to help the girls—whatever you want."

Greg nodded. "Sure thing, Chief."

Chapter Twenty

KRISTEN WAS GLAD TO SEE Nolan come back upstairs. She still had Mary Ann, Barbara, Kyle, Terry, and Chris all standing around talking a mile a minute. Maybe Nolan would get them the hell out of her kitchen. He looked pretty grim, so she wondered what he'd discovered. When the rest of them saw him, a hush fell over the group.

Nolan cleared his throat. "It looks like the gallery was burglarized last night. The only thing we know for sure was taken was the cash Mary Ann had left in the workroom as startup cash for today, which was about three hundred dollars. We would like to have the rest of the inventory examined to see if anything else was stolen."

Kyle said, "I was here until we closed last night so I can tell you if anything of mine is missing." He looked at Terry. "I assume you can do the same?"

Terry nodded. "Yeah and some of the other artisans will be arriving soon, so they can probably do the same with their stuff."

Mary Ann said, "The main area we won't know about is Kristen's since she wasn't here for the sale and... Oh my God. Is this why Farley got sick? Did someone poison him?"

Nolan grimaced. "It's entirely possible." Looking at Kristen he said, "You should probably call the vet and let him know what happened, in case he wants to run some additional tests for that."

Kristen's eyes filled with tears, but she nodded and presumably went to get her cell phone to call the vet.

Nolan said to the rest of them, "Please go down and try to figure out if anything else was stolen. Chief Macgregor said you can go ahead and open today if you feel up to it. Mary Ann, I'm going to leave that up to you, while I talk to Kristen. If you decide not to open, we need to let the chief know, so he can deal with the tourists coming in. We've got an hour before the express ferry gets here."

They all trooped down the stairs to do as asked while Nolan followed Kristen into the bedroom. She was just hanging up when he walked in. He went over, sat next to her on the bed, and put his arm around her, she curled into him.

She sniffed. "He said Farley is awake this morning and acting fine. There seems to be no lasting effects. He thinks it might have been sleeping pills or something like that. Why would anyone be mean enough to poison my dog?

For a measly three hundred dollars? I'd have given the jerk three hundred dollars not to hurt my dog."

"I know, baby."

"But to poison my sweet dog. This is why I hate living in town. People are assholes. All of them. Well, except you. And Chris. And Mary Ann. And a few other people aren't assholes, I guess, but still. Most of them are. Maybe not most, but some."

Nolan sighed. "I'm so sorry I wasn't here last night to protect you."

"I didn't really need protection. Seems like the guy is kind of a chicken shit if he ran off as soon as I flushed the toilet. I did kinda miss you in bed, however."

"It scared the crap out of me that you were here alone. What if he'd come upstairs with you here by yourself?"

"I'm not normally alone—I have Farley. Which, I suppose, is why he poisoned him. Or at least to keep him from barking, like he did the other nights. When I thought it was bears or raccoons, and I suppose it was the thief putting my trash cans upside down not you."

"I thought it was you."

"Kinda dumb of us not to put two and two together. And even with Farley we just didn't think about someone poisoning him. Which pisses me off. I mean, why couldn't the damn jerk find someone else to rob?"

"He has been."

"Oh, right. My turn, I guess. I hope you find the bastard and fry him. Poisoning my dog. I don't really give a shit about the money or even if he stole other things or tore up the gallery...."

"Which he didn't."

"But my dog... fucker."

Nolan rubbed her back. "The chief said Farley might have picked up his scent from the tainted food, if there was some, and might act differently toward him, so for you to pay attention."

She sat up straight and turned toward him. "Really? We should take Farley into town and let him look around. Once he gets back from Chelan."

Nolan frowned. "That might not be a bad idea. If he did act different toward someone we could at least fingerprint them and see if anything matches. We'll need to fingerprint you and Mary Ann and a few other people to see if we lifted any that don't match you guys."

"Fine. So, we should probably go down and help before the hordes arrive. Oh! Can we open?"

"Yes, if you and the rest feel up to it."

Kristen shrugged. "I don't know why not."

When they got downstairs, everything looked normal to Kristen.

Nolan took the notebook out of his pocket. "Was anything else taken?"

Mary Ann answered. "A few things maybe. For sure a large quilt, bed sized, not a real expensive one as they go, but since it was large it wasn't cheap either. Also, some candles and soaps maybe—we have a lot of them so we can't tell for sure—but it looked like some were missing from a table. There was a blank spot. All those things would be too unique to resell, here in town anyway. We were talking about it and wondered if they were for use by the person. It will be getting cooler at night soon so a blanket would make sense and candles and soap for obvious reasons."

"Good ideas, Mary Ann. Anything else taken?" Nolan asked.

"We didn't find anything else. Inventory seems to match what we expected to find."

Tim came over. "One more thing a small statue—pocket size really. I almost didn't bring it in 'cause it's kinda small and plain. It's just a cross."

Kristen asked, "A cross? Like a church kind of cross?"

Tim nodded. "Yeah one of my first carvings since it was easy. I brought it not so much to sell as for sentimental reasons—not sure it was on the inventory list or even priced."

"Interesting." Nolan looked at his watch. "The tourists will be walking in any minute, so I'm going to go back to work. Call me if you find anything else missing. I'll come by after my shift, to see if you need help."

As Nolan walked out the back door, tourists walked in the front.

Hours later as the last of the tourists left out the front, Nolan walked in the back door and brought with him the most delicious smell.

Kristen stopped mid-sentence. "Oh, my God, what is that smell?"

Nolan smirked. "Spaghetti and meatballs, garlic bread, and salad. Hungry?"

"Starved! I never took time to eat lunch and all I had this morning for breakfast, before the rush of craziness happened, was half a piece of toast and coffee."

Nolan laughed. "Then you better get a move on before the rest of your team beat you to it."

"I'd have to resort to violence, but instead I will just run ahead of them." And with that she was off like a shot.

Mary Ann got up to follow her, but just then the door opened and Trey walked in. She stopped mid-step, turned on her heel, and walked into his arms.

He laughed and swung her around. "I've got two days off, can you get some free time?"

Mary Ann looked at Nolan. "Please tell Kristen I got violently ill and will be back on Wednesday morning first thing."

Nolan shrugged. "Will do."

Mary Ann shoved the cash box in his hands and practically ran out the door with Trey.

Kristen walked back into the gallery with a ginormous plate of spaghetti and meatballs. Under the spaghetti plate was a large bowl Nolan assumed was salad, and garlic bread was perched precariously on top of the spaghetti.

She shoveled a huge bite into her mouth, chewed twice, and swallowed. Nolan just grinned at her while holding the cashbox.

"You are my hero—I was starving. Why are you holding the cashbox? Where's Mary Ann? I figured she was right behind me, since she started complaining about being hungry an hour ago."

Nolan said, "She's feeding a different kind of hunger."

"What do you mean?"

"Trey walked in right after you ran to the break room—knocking down children and old ladies in your haste. She took one look at him and told me to tell you she was going to be violently ill until Wednesday."

"Thank goodness he didn't come off the mountain earlier. Did he say anything about my place?"

Nolan shook his head. "She didn't even give him a chance to say hello, she just started dragging him out the door."

"*Hmm.* I wonder if any of the other guys came to town with him, or if I'm going to have to wait until Wednesday."

"I don't know about the other guys, but you won't be seeing Trey any time soon."

Terry, who created custom-designed furniture looked around the gallery. "You need some chairs in here, girlfriend." Then he sat on the floor and popped a meatball in his mouth.

Kristen swallowed the garlic bread she was inhaling, "Feel free to make me some. We'll let people sit on them until they sell. Some benches might be nice, too. Like for a yard or something."

Kyle sat next to Terry, "I could do a couple of benches— been thinking about trying some anyway. Metal is better for outdoors."

And with that, Kyle and Terry argued about wood versus metal, while everyone else ate. Not that the argument stopped them from eating. When there was no food left they all restocked the store for Monday.

Terry called out, "Hey, Kristen, can you come here a sec?"

"What is it?" she said when she got over to where he was. Nolan followed her.

"I found some things not priced," he said and held out a sculpture.

Kristen took it from him and turned it over in her hands. It was a carving of a bear which was very detailed and carved from rock. "I've never seen this before, but it's amazing."

"That's what I thought, which is why I was looking to see how much it is. I was thinking about buying it. And then I saw some others. Look. None of them are priced—I checked."

She and Nolan turned to the table where Terry pointed, and on it, interspersed with other things, were a dozen rock carvings. All of nature and all beautifully done. "Amazing, Mary Ann must have taken them in and forgot to price them. I would call her to ask, but I don't think she'll be answering her phone until Wednesday. I guess I'll price them and we can figure it out later."

Nolan helped her get the mini sculptures priced. All the restocking was done and people were ready to leave. She said goodbye to everyone.

"Call if you need us, but I think Monday should be much quieter. Otherwise gonna stay home and make up some chairs and benches," Terry said with a look at Kyle.

Kyle smirked back at Terry. "You can call me too, Kristen. Otherwise, I'll be working on benches. Unless I get a real estate call."

Terry punched Kyle in the arm and Kyle punched him back, then they both laughed like loons and walked out the door together, probably heading to Greg's bar for a beer.

Kristen shook her head. "You would think that by now they would have outgrown that—but boys will be boys, I suppose."

Chapter Twenty-One

THERE WAS ONLY ONE WAY Nolan was going to be leaving Kristen's tonight and that was if she was going with him, to his house. He knew he was being irrational; it was highly unlikely the thief would come back to her house again, but he just didn't give a crap that he was being ridiculous—he was not leaving her until the dog was back to cause a ruckus if the perp came back. Nolan was also going to check every frickin' door and window and make sure the damn things were shut and locked.

Chris had put the screen back on the window and cleaned up the garbage. He'd put the trashcans back where they were supposed to have been all along and once he'd pointed that out to Nolan, he felt even stupider for not noticing they were missing from where they were supposed to be. How in the hell had he missed all the clues? That was pretty damn obvious—his dick had been leading him around whenever he got within a hundred yards of Kristen.

So, how could he be with her, protect her, and not be completely stupid around her? That was the real question. Could he just hang out and have a platonic relationship with her? He could give it a try.

Kristen looked up after counting out the money she wanted to put into the night deposit. "I need to take this to the bank, since Mary Ann left skid marks on her way to go jump Trey. Want to come with me?"

Nolan nodded. "It would probably be best for two people to do the deposit anyway—just to be on the safe side."

Kristen smirked. "Okay, Officer Thompson, whatever you think is best, sir."

Nolan didn't crack a smile. He needed to put some distance in their relationship so he could keep her safe. "Good, I'm going to check all the doors and windows. Then, we can get going."

Kristen's smile faded. "I think I'll call the vet and check on Farley while you do that."

She looked so sad he squeezed her shoulder as he walked past her to check on the locks. Once he'd reassured himself everything was secured, he went back to her.

"The vet says Farley is doing fine and he agrees it was probably some kind of sleeping pill, since there has been no other sign of trouble."

"Good. So, you are going into Chelan tomorrow to get him. What's the plan then?"

Kristen said, "I'll have to work the gallery in the morning since Mary Ann is *violently ill* and take either the express or the late ferry into Chelan, depending on how many customers show up tomorrow. I will probably just spend the night there and come back on the express in the morning. Tammy can open and I'll be back with any tourists coming on the ferry, so I think that will work."

"Sounds like a good plan."

"Want to come with me?" Kristen purred.

Nolan shook his head. "Have to work Monday and Tuesday. My next day off is Wednesday."

"Oh, okay then. So, do you want to try taking Farley into town?"

"I would, yes. Since Mary Ann will be over her *illness* on Wednesday, how about we go together to walk him around for a while? Let's try early, since it seems our thief is nocturnal he might still be out early in the morning. If that doesn't work, let's also try later in the evening."

"Sounds good. I need some time to work in my studio. This gallery opening has put me behind schedule on a few things. Fortunately, my customers are not in a rush for anything right now."

Nolan asked, "So, you can do that mid-day in between our Farley walks?"

"Yes, exactly."

Nolan said, "Ready to go to the bank?"

"Yes, want to stop by Greg's after we do that for a beer?"

Nolan decided maybe being with other people would help him maintain his distance, so he agreed. "That sounds nice. I could use a cold one."

"Yeah, it's been a hell of a weekend."

WHEN THEY WALKED into Greg's bar they saw a few of the hotshots at a table. Kristen waved to Greg who nodded and then she walked over to the wildland firefighters. They seemed to be in a pretty intense conversation about a shack they had found in a remote area, so she just waited patiently until they noticed her.

"Hey, guys."

One of the hotshots, Kevin she thought, jumped up and grabbed her in a bear hug. "Hey guys, this is the lady who saved our asses by not leaving those A5 tanks at that house on the ridge."

The other firefighters shot to their feet and passed her around, each one giving her a hug nearly squeezing the life out of her. One, who was apparently the chief, said, "We can't thank you enough for that ma'am—and we also want to thank you for letting us use your house as a base of operations. We've kept it safe."

"I'm glad it's safe and the only reason I didn't leave is I couldn't move the damn things myself."

"Yeah, nearly a couple hundred pounds is a little over *do it yourself* weight, even for a man. But, we do appreciate you staying and waiting for someone to show up to help you. A half dozen of those things getting too hot in a fire and it would have blown the whole top of the mountain off—and all of us with it."

Kristen blushed. "So, how is the fire going up there?"

The chief replied, "Not great. We get some of it out and then the wind picks up and moves it to the next spot. Or, we have more dry lightning that starts a new area. I don't think it'll be out before the first snow."

"That's fine, I'm settled in town for now. So, what were you talking about when I walked up? Something about a shack?"

The chief said, "Oh you might be the perfect person to ask. So, a couple of miles from your location we found a shack. Looks like someone lived there for years. It was burned to the ground, but there was an extensive garden and an area dug out that looked like a meat locker. Looked like there had been some chickens too. Do you know who it might belong to?"

Kristen shook her head.

Nolan, who had been standing back listening to the exchange stepped forward. "Officer Nolan Thompson. Can you give me more information about that and we can see if we can track the person down?"

"Sure, officer. Have a seat you two."

Greg brought them over a couple beers and Kristen watched Nolan become all cop, as he took down the information the fire fighters told him, about the cabin that had burned. She found it fascinating to see her calm, easy-going lover turn into a cop with cold eyes and quiet authority. He asked questions and took notes in the little notebook she didn't even realize he carried around with him. When he had all the information they had to share, he sat back, picked up his beer, and transformed back into the laid-back guy.

The hotshots laughed and told stories about their work—their deadly work—up on the mountain fighting fire and trying to avoid scared wild animals. After an hour and a half, Kristen and Nolan decided it was time to get back. They said goodnight to their new friends and waved to Greg.

On the drive back Nolan said, "So, you've never seen anyone up by your place that might stay in that cabin."

"No. Never."

"I wonder…"

"What?"

"You've never had any problems with a thief in town, have you?"

Kristen shook her head. "Other than the occasional kid stealing a candy bar, not that I've ever been aware of."

Nolan nodded. "That's what I thought. So, suppose that this person who lives off the grid and no one has ever met, gets burned out of his home. What's he going to do to survive if he's not able to come into town to work?"

Kristen gasped. "So, you think our thief might be that guy? That he can't just come into town and get a job or a new place to live so he's stealing? That would explain the blanket and soap and candles. What's he stolen from the other businesses?"

"Good question. I didn't pay a lot of attention to what he stole in the previous burglaries—just the total dollar amount, to see if it was felony or misdemeanor. I know food was stolen from Amber's and the grocery store, but that's about all they have, so I didn't think about it much. I think I'll check into that when I get into work, first thing tomorrow."

They got to her house and Nolan parked and turned off the car. Then he turned in the seat toward her. "I don't want you to be alone until Farley gets back to be your alarm."

"Of course. You're welcome to stay."

"I was thinking I should sleep in your guest room."

"What? Why?"

"So I'm not distracted and can actually guard you as opposed to being your lover."

Kristen frowned. "But, I don't really want a guard. Do you really think the guy will come back? Didn't you lock all the windows?"

"Yes, I did. And no, I don't think he'd risk the same location a second night, but I just think it would be better if we sleep in different rooms."

"Fine, but I don't want to hear any whining in the morning about being lonely or horny. You just blew it buddy." And then she slammed out of the car and marched up the stairs.

Nolan watched her go and wanted desperately to call her back or run after her and beg her forgiveness, but her safety was more important. He couldn't risk getting distracted and her getting hurt. He just couldn't do it. So, he followed slowly, locking the door behind him and carrying his duffle of clothes, to her guest room. He got undressed and got into bed. He heard her slamming around in her room. She was not happy with him.

KRISTEN WAS SO pissed off it wasn't even funny. She'd finally let some man into her life and now he was rejecting her? Well, fuck that. And then to blame it on wanting to keep her safe. Right. Like she was some ditzy girl who couldn't take care of herself. She lived on top of a mountain all by herself, with just her dog for company. She could chop down trees and split them into firewood. She could hunt and fish—and then clean the game and process it for food. She could chase off bears and mountain lions. She could change the oil in her truck and the brakes too, thank you very much. She wasn't some debutante that needed a big strong man to protect her from the scaries.

Too pissed off to relax, she stalked out of her room, got her water bottle filled and went out the backdoor to her workroom. Nolan, the big strong man, could sleep while she went down to her studio and got some work done. She locked Nolan in, so nothing would get him.

Nolan sat on his bed, tormented because Kristen was angry with him. Finally, she seemed to get over it and was quiet. He waited a few minutes to see if she started back up again—he didn't think she was the type of woman who got over being mad quickly. He hoped she wasn't in her room crying now. What if she was? Should he check on her? Maybe. He got up off the bed and quietly went down the hall to her room. It was very dark in the corridor, he could hardly see her door; he should have left his bedroom door open for some light.

He leaned toward it to see if he could hear anything. Nope. Not a sound. Just silence. Too quiet? He leaned in closer and bumped his shoulder on the door, it pushed open.

"Kristen? Sorry. Didn't mean to bother you."

All he heard was…nothing—no response at all. She couldn't be asleep that quick; he'd slept with her on several occasions and she didn't drift off instantly. He went into the room and stood next to the bed. There was a bit of light coming from the window and he could see the bed was empty and still made. Maybe she was taking a shower. He turned toward the master bath that connected to her room, but the door was open and it was dark. Where was she? He looked outside and saw the light on in the studio.

Shit. He was in her house to protect her and she'd walked outside *alone* to go to the studio. Was she crazy? He wasn't going to put up with that nonsense for one minute. He stormed into his room, pulled on his jeans and got his shoes and gun. Then he stomped over to the door. She had the keys so he couldn't lock the deadbolt. Dammit. Well, he'd just have to leave it unlocked—but he put a tiny piece of paper in it so he could see if it was opened after he left. Crazy frickin' woman, it would be just his luck some perp would get into the house while the door was locked by the flimsy handle.

He marched down the stairs and over to the studio. She had sound blaring—angry music. Guess she was still pissed off at him. Clearly they were both pissed. The door was locked when he tried it. Well, great. Just great. He wasn't sure she'd even hear him if he knocked or pounded on the door. When the music quieted a bit, he slammed his fist against the wood. A few seconds later the music stopped and she opened the door.

"What do you want? You just made me screw up a cut with your knocking."

"What are you doing out here? I stayed at your house to keep you safe. I can't do that if you're out here."

Kristen crossed her arms. "I don't need a fucking bodyguard. I don't *want* a fucking bodyguard. I can take care of myself. I'm not some prima donna that needs you to keep her safe. I'm too pissed off to sleep, so I decided to get some work done. I'm behind on several projects."

"But I told you—"

She poked him in the chest. "You." *Poke.* "Don't." *Poke.* "Own." *Poke.* "Me." *Poke.*

Nolan grabbed her hand. "I'm not trying to own you. I'm trying to keep you safe and think with my head, instead of my dick."

Kristen wrenched her hand back from him and put her hands on her hips. "I like the way your dick thinks better than your head."

Then she must've realized what she'd said and so did he. They looked at each other. She blinked. And he blinked. And then, they both burst into laughter.

"I can't believe you said that." He guffawed.

She snorted. "I can't believe I did either."

"The way my dick thinks…" He chortled.

"Better than your head." She cackled.

"Only you, Kristen. Only you," he said, wiping tears from his eyes.

"Special, aren't I?" she said holding her stomach.

"Yes, you are *very* special," Nolan said and the chuckles dissipated into heat. "I'm sorry. I was trying to be responsible. When I realized we had seen the evidence of someone trying to break in for two weeks and I just didn't put two and two together, I felt like a damn fool. I'm supposed to be a police officer and be observant. But, I have been so enthralled with you since the first day on the mountain, I'm just not thinking clearly."

"Oh, Nolan. We had a logical excuse for all of them. How could you know to try to put them together?"

"We did have other break-ins…."

She put her hand over his mouth. "*Shh*. Don't beat

yourself up over it. You'll find the guy—maybe with Farley's help on Wednesday."

"So, are you really going to work now?"

Kristen looked him in the eye. "Are you really going to sleep in the guest room?"

"If you promise not to work, I promise to not sleep in the guest room."

"Good, let's go to bed."

"Do you need to clean up in here?" he asked, looking around.

"No, I was too pissed off to really work and was just chopping scrap metal into bits."

He laughed and she took his hand before they walked out of the studio and locked it. When they got to the top of the stairs she stared at the door.

She whispered, "What if someone...."

He plucked the tiny paper out of the door and said, "No worries."

After they locked the door behind them, they went directly to her room where they undressed each other and then took a long time before going to sleep. A very long time.

Chapter Twenty-Two

NOLAN LEFT EARLY THE next morning. He wanted time to look over the burglary files before he started his shift. He got to the office and got out the information he wanted. There had been a break-in at Amber's restaurant where food and some plates, coffee cups, knives, and a couple of pans had been taken—and they thought maybe some toilet paper and paper towels. Food, again, from the tiny grocery store. There had been a burglary at the tourist shop where some T-shirts, sweats, and—again—food had been stolen. At the drug store, which was really an all-purpose store, there had been a fishing pole and bait box missing, plus some camping equipment—a small tent, a sleeping bag and a small lantern. Yep, the guy was setting up a living space and replacing a few necessary items. The fishing pole would mean he was by one of the two rivers bordering the town.

Nolan was eager to meet with the rest of the guys to talk about what he'd learned. He sent out a text mentioning he thought he had a breakthrough and could anyone that was available come in for a briefing before shift. He got a 10-4 from all of them—even the off-duty guys. He made a fresh pot of coffee and wondered if he should run over to Samantha's for some pastries, when Ben texted him to say he was going to do that very thing.

Nolan went into the conference room and started writing on the whiteboard each of the locations that had been burglarized and what had been taken. He also put a pin in the map of the area where the hotshots had said the camp had been found—fortunately, the fire chief had the coordinates in the notebook he carried, so they had a very accurate location. It was nowhere near the road so if the guy did come into town he'd have a big hike to do so. It looked like the guy really lived completely off the grid in the wilderness. He couldn't imagine anyone doing that, and if they did were they stable enough to be in town? He wondered what would drive someone to such extremes.

When they all had coffee and a pastry they assembled in the conference room. Nolan stood up. "Some of the hotshots were in town last night and were talking about a cabin they found a few miles off the road in a very rugged un-mapped area. The cabin was highly established with a large garden and rabbit hutches, but was also well hidden in trees and brush. The hotshots were asking Kristen if she'd ever seen anyone, and it got me to thinking about the break-ins—that maybe the person breaking in was displaced by the fire. So, I came in this morning and looked through the files. You can see on the whiteboard the things that have been stolen and in the order they were stolen.

Chief Macgregor looked at Nolan. "It looks like we know why the person is stealing—good job. The sizes of the sweats stolen were a man's small so he's not a big person. Which was also indicated by the windows he's been going in through."

Ben said, "Maybe we should ask around. See if anyone saw someone that looked homeless."

Nolan nodded. "Kristen will have Farley back on Wednesday and we thought to take him around town and see if he acted different toward anyone. He might have a scent from the tainted food."

"Good. Well, men, we know more now than we did. Let's see if we can find this guy and wrap this up. Nolan and Ben—while you're on duty today go back to the places broken into and ask about them seeing a smallish homeless person. The rest of you, as you go about your day, feel free to mention it to anyone you talk to. And everyone, keep your eyes open."

As the room disbursed the chief asked Nolan to come to his office for a minute. Chief James sat behind his desk. "Close the door and have a seat."

Nolan closed the door as asked, wondering if he was in trouble—he was already disgusted with himself for not putting so many clues together before now.

"Nolan, I appreciate you taking the initiative in this case and bringing us together with that briefing. That is exactly the kind of officer I'm looking for. Have you heard about the mayoral election coming up next summer?"

"Yes, sir. It seems like the main topic of conversation around town. Even more so than the fires and robberies."

"Good. One of the reasons I brought you and Juan into the department is to find a replacement for myself. I'm planning to run for mayor and I need a police chief to take my place. Ben's not interested and the other guys aren't seasoned enough—which is why I went outside our community for new officers. Juan is solid and does a good job, but he doesn't take a lot of initiative to go beyond his daily work. You, on the other hand, took the initiative to come in early this morning. You talked to the hotshots last night, and you plan to use your day off to take Kristen's dog around town to see how he acts."

"But, I had a lot of the evidence right in my face at Kristen's and I missed it completely."

"I didn't say I was looking for someone perfect, I'm looking for someone who cares enough to put in a few extra hours and has a good head on his shoulders. I'm not ready to name you chief, but I want you to think about it. If you are interested, I'd like you to take a few online courses and I'd want to start working with you to familiarize you with my role. Think about it for a few days and we can talk more about it then."

"Thank you, sir, for thinking about me. I'll give it some thought."

"Good. Now, go out and see if you can find this guy."

Nolan walked out of the room stunned. He'd had no

idea that was coming. Police chief. Was he really ready for that? He really didn't know what all it might entail. Online classes would be fine. Shadowing the chief would also be fine. But, *being* the chief? That would take some getting used to. He supposed part of the job would be to take a more active part in the town. Like going to town council meetings and things like that. Which he could probably handle, too. He could think about it later—right now he had people to interview. He sent Ben a text to divvy up the locations and headed out to talk to people.

KRISTEN GOT UP when Nolan left and decided she'd spend some time in the studio before the gallery would be officially open. She didn't really think they would have a large crowd today since it was a workday, so Tammy could probably handle it. Kristen would keep herself available just in case.

When she got to the studio she first cleaned up the mess she'd made last night by chopping the scrap metal into bits. It would all just go back into the scrap metal container she kept to melt down anyway. So, it didn't hurt anything for her to have her little temper tantrum.

She decided to finish up a few pieces she had almost ready for sale. She could either put them in her gallery or ship them off to another one outside of town, where she always had good sales. She also needed to work on setting a couple of stones for her friend in Colorado who wanted a matching necklace and ring set. It was a simple design and all that was needed was to set the stones and polish up the pieces. She had a fairly ornate piece for Vangie she was working on, so if she had time, she wanted to try to put in some effort on that one too.

She got in a good three hours of solid work and then realized the gallery would be opening in ten minutes. So, she closed up the studio and went to the house. Tammy was there, all ready for the day. She called out *hello* to her and went to go see if she needed to put out a few more of her pieces. She decided they would be good as long as they didn't have a huge rush.

She heard the door chime and went toward the front as over a dozen women streamed in. Oh, for God's sake, how long were they going to be inundated? She plastered on a smile and went forward to greet the customers.

THE LAST PERSON ON his list to talk to today was Kristen, so he grabbed a couple of sandwiches from Amber's and headed over there. He figured he could take his lunch break and talk at the same time—and he was pretty sure she would not have eaten. He'd looked in her fridge this morning and a mouse would have starved to death on what she had on hand. Plenty of condiments, but not a darn thing to put them on. The woman needed a keeper.

He parked in back and walked into the gallery—and couldn't believe how full it was. As far as he could see, it was only Kristen and Tammy running the place. Shit. He'd have to talk to her another time, the place was a zoo.

He went over to Tammy and handed her a sandwich. "Go eat quick. I'll man the money."

"Oh, thank you, Nolan. You are a lifesaver. I've been starving and we've had non-stop people. First it was a church group from Chelan and then a book club from Mason and then—"

Nolan interrupted, "Go eat now. I don't have a long time that I can stay and I want Kristen to eat, too. We don't want her to get *hangry*."

Tammy laughed and hurried to the break room. Nolan started taking money and wrapping things up for transport on the ferry.

Tammy was back in twenty minutes. "I hurried. Get some food into Kristen."

He high-fived Tammy and left her with the cash box to find Kristen surrounded by women.

Nolan cleared his throat and in his best Barry White voice said, "Ladies how can I help you, while we let Kristen have a bite of lunch."

Kristen smiled at him weakly.

"Oh, but we're artists and are asking Kristen about her art," said one enthusiastic woman in turquoise glasses and a red and purple sundress.

"Oh, well, I'm a glass artist and would be happy to tell you all about the glass sculptures and how to make them," he said pointing to his mother's art on the other side of the gallery. "Let's move over there."

As they all started in that direction, he handed off the other sandwich to Kristen. "You are going to owe me."

"Thanks. If you can get rid of them before I can scarf this down, I'll pay you double."

Nolan grinned. "A challenge I will work hard to meet."

When Kristen came back from eating the sandwich, she couldn't believe her eyes—all those women crafters were gone. Hallelujah.

She went over to Nolan who was watching them walk down the steps heading toward her sister's boutique. If Barbara knew what was good for her she'd hide in her office and lock the door. Kristen thought maybe she should call her and warn her. Then again, no one had called to warn her, so fair was fair.

Nolan turned from the window and grinned. "You owe me double."

"What did you do? Threaten to arrest them?"

"No need for that. I just pointed out that the quilter worked in the next building over and maybe steered them toward a few of the other artists like Kyle and Terry—and told them if they hurried they could talk to all of them before the ferry left. I drew them a nice little map on how to manage to see them all, while arriving back on time at the landing."

Kristen gasped in horror. "Oh no, they're going to be on the same ferry as I am?"

"Yeah. So, I was thinking maybe you should figure out a disguise before you got on board."

"Nothing short of a *Jason* mask would deter them—and even then they might ask him how he learned to kill people so artfully."

Nolan laughed. "They did seem to be curious about every aspect."

"Do you really think they were crafters or artists?"

"No, I used my superior deduction skills as a trained police officer to determine that they might get together once a week to work on pre-made kits. But, that's about the extent of it."

Kristen smiled. "And just how did you determine that?"

"I mentioned that you really liked your new titanium torch and how you were seeing that titanium burned so much cleaner than acetylene."

Kristen snorted. "But titanium is…."

"A metal. Yes, I know—which is why when two of them agreed with me and said they were also enjoying their new torches…."

Kristen laughed a full belly laugh. "You are so bad."

"But, no one would ever expect that from my innocent boyish face." Nolan grinned.

Kristen snorted again. "Boyish? Innocent? Hardly. Those are two words I'd never use to describe you."

The radio on Nolan's shoulder crackled. "One sec, Kristen." Keying the mic, he said, "Officer Thompson." He listened. "10-4. On my way."

Kristen took his hand when he turned back toward her. "Thanks for saving me and bringing me food. I'll see you on Wednesday—or if you want to come by Tuesday night that would be better."

"I'll look forward to it. I'll bring a pizza or something. You won't want to cook just getting back from Chelan, plus the fact you have no food."

Kristen shrugged. Food wasn't always high on her list of priorities. "I have ice cream."

"I must have missed that. Gotta go."

Kristen grinned as he left, then she thought about going on the ferry with all those irritating women and wondered if maybe she should move to Iceland, or get a big iguana for a pet to keep them at bay.

NOLAN SPRINTED OUT to jump in his car to head over to Amber's. Ben was talking to her during her after-lunch lull about seeing a homeless person and he thought she had some information to share. Since he hadn't gotten any of the sandwiches he'd given Kristen and Tammy, he rooted around in the car and found a package of Junior Mints he inhaled. Maybe he could grab something from Amber's after they talked to her. He wondered what her special was for the day.

One of the women crafters had made him want some jambalaya. She had a Cajun accent and it reminded him of the excellent food he'd eaten in New Orleans. His mother once had a showing of her art there and the whole family had gone to it. What an experience that had been—he and his sister had been in awe of everything. Those were some good memories.

He pulled up in front of the restaurant and went in to find Ben and Amber seated at a table near the salad bar. Both had plates of food in front of them. *Score!* The waitress asked if he wanted anything and he gave her his order. They had a hot turkey sandwich as the special and his mouth watered at the thought, pushing the jambalaya to the back of his mind.

The waitress brought him a Coke and said his order would be ready in a jiffy. He sat down at the table after grabbing some salad. "I'm so glad you guys are eating—I'm starving."

Ben frowned. "I thought you were on lunch break before."

"I was, but I went to Kristen's gallery to have lunch with her and the place was packed, so I took turns letting both Tammy and Kristen have a lunch break and eat my sandwiches. Otherwise, they were not going to get food *or* a break. Which also means I didn't get a chance to talk to Kristen. She's going on the ferry to get Farley back tonight, so I'll have to ask her about spotting homeless people tomorrow night."

"Well, aren't you Mr. Self-sacrifice."

Amber said, "Be nice, Ben, and eat your lunch."

Nolan ignored Ben's jibe and shoveled in some salad. "So, tell me what you saw Amber."

"I'm not sure, but yesterday a young person came in. I can't really tell how old he was because he had a very weathered face—like someone who spent way too much time outside, with no sunscreen. But he was kind of on the small side, so I was trying to decide if he was a small adult or a teenager. He didn't read the menu just looked around at what people near him were eating and said 'I want that' and pointed to the hamburger plate one of the customers next to him had. Which I thought was odd, because even if you can't read, you generally know what a hamburger is. He ordered one and wolfed it down like someone was going to take it from him. Then, when he came up to the register to pay, he just handed me a wad of money—which ended up being like fifty dollars. I took what I needed and gave him the change and he walked out without tipping the waitress. Which happened to be me, so I knew he had the money to do it."

"Can you describe him?"

"Yes. He had longish brown hair with a touristy baseball cap. Blue eyes, no beard—which might be a clue to his age. A long, straight nose and crooked teeth. He definitely could use an orthodontist."

The waitress brought Nolan his food and although

he was starving, Amber's story had him intrigued. He thanked the waitress and nodded at Amber to continue while he cut into the turkey.

Amber said, "He was about my height which is five foot-five and with a slight build, but with large muscles which confused the age thing again. He was very muscly through the chest and arms and legs too, from what I could see. He had on a T-shirt with a picture of Lake Chelan on it and buckskin pants and moccasins. Very odd clothing."

"Did you notice which way he went?"

"No, I was busy running the register and waitressing at the same time—one of my staff had called in with the brown bottle flu, I think. Too much of a good time with the firefighters at Greg's is my guess."

Nolan took another bite of his turkey sandwich dripping in gravy, thinking while he chewed. "This is delicious. So, did he get a soda or dessert?"

"No, just drank several glasses of water. He didn't use any ketchup or even salt anything that I saw. Just ate everything on his plate—including the parsley. Not many people eat the parsley."

"Did he talk to you much? What did he sound like?" Nolan scooped up a big bite of turkey and bread and mashed potatoes.

"He really didn't talk a lot. He pointed out what he wanted and used few words. But, he didn't seem standoffish exactly—just not chatty. He did seem interested in watching people around him. I didn't really notice an accent or anything like that."

Ben said around a mouthful of hamburger, "Tell him about the utensils."

"Right. He didn't use any. He ate everything with his hands."

Nolan shrugged. "A hamburger and French fries...."

"No, not French fries. The person he pointed out had a hamburger and side salad. He ate the salad with his fingers, too. And didn't really use his napkin much, at least at first—he used it more at the end of the meal. Which I noticed because when he was eating the salad he didn't use it, but at the end when he was getting ready to leave he did."

"Interesting."

Amber clasped her hands in front of her chest. "So, do you think it might be the guy?"

"It might be, but we cannot go by speculation," Nolan said. "If he comes back in, give us a call, okay?"

"Yes. I will," she said and took a big bite of her French dip sandwich which was probably getting cold.

Ben picked up some French fries. "I wish we had a police sketch artist."

Nolan nodded. "That would be nice. I could try, but drawing people is not my skill set. I could get a rough sketch though, I suppose."

"Oh. I guess you must have some talent drawing—being Lucille's son—it never occurred to me. But, I'm sure Barbara could do a sketch, drawing people and their clothes are her forte," Amber said.

Ben looked up and rubbed his chin. "Yeah, she probably could."

"Really? Amber, can you work with her on that? We might be able to pay for her time."

Amber shook her head. "Oh, she wouldn't want payment—but yes I'll go over and work with her to see if we can come up with a good likeness."

Nolan lifted a shoulder. "Good. See if she can do both a close-up head shot and a full body with his clothes."

"Clothes are her specialty."

They all three finished their lunch and Ben and Nolan paid Amber before they walked out front. Nolan stopped Ben with a hand on his arm. "Good job. I think you may be on to something."

Ben smiled. "Thanks. I thought it sounded promising."

"It does, and I'm glad we have something to go on now."

"Yeah, unless he steals some jeans and shoes, those buckskin pants and moccasins are going to be dead giveaways."

Kristen got on the ferry and tried to find a place to hide from the women. She'd brought along a magazine to hide behind and had picked a secluded corner to sit in. Unfortunately, she had not thought through the hiding thing, because it actually brought her more attention since she'd chosen *Lapidary Journal Jewelry Artist*. Dumb, dumb,

dumb. Couldn't she have picked anything else, other than a jewelry designers magazine? Good grief. Nothing like waving a red flag.

The women zeroed in on her and she spent the entire ride on the ferry downlake trapped by the crafters. She got off at the first landing, assuming the ladies would get off at the last one. She didn't care if she had to walk into Chelan—she couldn't stand one more minute with those people. Thank God. They did stay on the ferry, but they promised her they would be back to her gallery soon. She hoped she'd be in Iceland or Hawaii or Singapore.

She got a ride to the vet and was glad to see her dog looking great and so happy to see her. The vet said there was no poison found in his system, but there had been a high concentration of fungus—as in mushrooms. So, they had deducted that he'd eaten some poisonous toadstools. They checked to make sure there was not any other side effects, since some plants were very lethal. But the vet thought he'd be fine and would have no lasting issues from it, since he'd voided his stomach before falling asleep.

She and Farley walked over to the hotel she'd booked for their night in Chelan. It was close to the ferry dock and an easy walk to restaurants and a park where she could take him.

Chapter Twenty-Three

KRISTEN TOOK THE EXPRESS ferry back to Chedwick from Chelan. She had her dog and a nice pile of groceries. She wasn't going to let Nolan give her a hard time about having no food again. At least not for a few days. She often forgot to order provisions and almost never took the time to go to the tiny market they had in town. The tourist prices were enough to discourage any of the locals from shopping there. So, she often had a bare refrigerator and cupboards. When it got bad enough she'd rouse herself to order groceries or eat out.

She filled up her car with the food, the dog, the small duffle she'd taken a change of clothes in, and she was off to help with the gallery. Not a lot of people got off the ferry in Chedwick, and the ones that did seemed to be families. Maybe they were headed to the amusement park—she could use a quiet day at the shop and Mary Ann would not be back until tomorrow, that rat. Although she'd probably be in a darn good mood when she did show up, after spending two days in bed with a hot fireman.

Kristen checked in with Tammy before hauling the groceries up the back stairs and putting it all away. She decided to leave Farley in the house rather than the yard, so he'd not be vulnerable to any evil people trying to poison him. She set her phone to remind her to go let him out every few hours and went down to the gallery. There were only a couple of people milling around so she took out a clipboard and checked each area trying to see what she needed to restock. Maybe she could get Tammy to make some phone calls this afternoon for more inventory.

The standard ferry brought a few more people to the gallery, but nothing the two of them couldn't handle—and they even managed to have lunch. No need for Nolan to rescue them today. She was looking forward to seeing him tonight; she should have offered to cook, but at the time she really hadn't had much food in the house. Now she did, so maybe she would cook for him later, since they were going to be taking Farley out to see if he could find the person who poisoned him with evil mushrooms. She hoped they would catch the guy, so she didn't have to worry about her dog.

When Tim showed up for the afternoon shift, she was happy to leave the gallery in his hands. The ferries were gone so that would just leave the tourists staying in town and any locals that wanted to come in. Tim could handle it and he brought his carvings to work on during any lulls they had.

She let Farley out and then went up to put on a sundress so she looked a little pretty for Nolan. She fluffed her hair and even put on some eyeshadow, perfume, and lip-gloss, which was a lot of primping for her. She wasn't much of a girly girl, so she never got crazy with makeup and hair. She rarely even wore her own jewelry—which was kind of silly of her, but she never really thought about it much.

Okay. She was ready. All she had to do was wait for Nolan to show up with pizza—knowing his routine he'd be there in about twenty minutes. So, she startled just a bit when someone knocked on the door. When she opened it, he was standing there with a grin and a pizza.

"You're early," she said.

At the same time, he said, "I hurried."

They laughed and he came in, set down the pizza, and dragged her into his arms. "I missed you."

"I was only gone one night."

"Yeah, but it was a really long night. In fact, I haven't seen you in nearly twenty-nine hours."

She grinned at him. "Silly man. Now give me a kiss."

He wrapped his arms around her waist and she put her hands around the back of his neck. They met in a full body embrace. She tilted her face up toward his and he leaned down to kiss the corner of her mouth, then he nibbled his way across her lips with tiny touches. Tingles shot through her from her face down to her toes. Finally, he set his mouth on hers and she opened to him and they devoured each other with long wet kisses and lots of heat.

"*Mmm*. Much better than pizza," he said.

"Yes, but if we don't stop and eat it will get cold and pizza is better hot."

Nolan pouted. "If you insist."

"I do, but then we can have more kisses for dessert."

"That works."

He got out two beers while she got plates, forks, and napkins.

Nolan whistled. "Whoa, there is actual food in your fridge."

"Don't get sassy with me. I just had extra time on my hands, so I did some shopping in Chelan. If you're nice I might make you an egg or two in the morning."

"I can be nice. So, how did it go on the ferry? Did the crafters recognize you?"

"Yes, dammit. I took a magazine to hide behind, but I wasn't thinking and took a lapidary magazine. No one reads those, but jewelers, so they caught me. And do you know what one of them asked me? I had to get off at the first Chelan dock, so I didn't kill her."

"But, the vet is at the other end of town… What did she ask?"

"She asked me what stamp I use for the flowers on that red jasper set. I don't use a damn stamp! I cut out each petal, each leaf, each stem with a jeweler's saw, thank-you very much. Stamp my ass. A stamp doesn't leave clean edges and it would all be one flower pattern not individual ones. I drill a tiny hole for each petal and then put a tiny blade into that hole and hand cut each petal. Stupid woman. I felt like punching her in the nose. Stamp."

"Okay, then. Sorry I brought it up. Here, eat your pizza."

While they ate, he told her about the clues they had discovered about the burglar.

Kristen stopped eating and just stared at him for a long moment.

"What?" he asked. "Do I have sauce on my face?"

"I think I saw him too."

"The thief?"

"Yes, the first day we were open. There was a young guy in here that was dressed a little raggedy. He was watching Mary Ann take the money for different things. I went over and asked if I could help him. He said something like, 'No gotta go.' Then, he nearly ran out the door. I kind of followed him out and he took off down the street. But, he wasn't going toward the ferry, so I tried to holler at him that he was going the wrong way, but he just ran faster."

"*Hmm*. Not toward the ferry, so down the street toward the outskirts of town?"

"Yes. Which, at the time, I just thought he was lost— but if he was going back to his camp that would make more sense."

"Good. Barbara is drawing up what Amber saw and once we get the drawing you can look and see if it's the same guy. If it is, maybe we can poke around in the direction you saw him go. One of the things he stole was a fishing pole, so we think he might be near a river. But we didn't know which one to focus on. With your sighting, we can go that direction first."

"Good. And if we can get the drawing before we take Farley out, that would be helpful too. If Farley can pick up his essence, and if it's the same guy, that would be more proof."

"Circumstantial, but still, better than nothing."

"But, if he's wearing stolen clothes...." Kristen said.

"Kinda hard to tell with clothes, especially tourist clothes, if he stole them or bought them."

"Oh, true."

"But, added all together it will be good to at least bring him in for questioning, or to see if we can find his camp where there would possibly be the quilt, which is the most unique item. That and the cross Tim carved," Nolan said.

Kristen nodded. "Yeah, that quilt was kind of unique with a large emerald-colored flower in the middle made out of different fabrics. So, in other words, you gather evidence, little by little."

"That's the way of most investigations."

"It would be nice if you could just flat out know for sure, like with something really incriminating."

Nolan shrugged. "Yes, but he's either very smart and keeping his thefts generic or he simply needs those items. I have to admit I am intrigued by his story. He doesn't seem to be your normal, everyday thief."

"True, but enough of all this. I'm going to clean up

our dinner. Can you let Farley out? Then we can find something more entertaining to do."

"Happy to, my sweet."

When they came back together, Nolan asked, "So what did you have in mind for something more entertaining to do?"

"Hmph. Well, if you can't think of anything...."

"Ah, throwing down the gauntlet, are you now? How about this?" He grabbed her, whirled her around, pressed her up against the wall, and covered her body with his. He put his hands on her elbows and brought her up on her toes, to cover her mouth in a kiss so hot she thought she might burst into flames right there.

But she gave as good as she got and their tongues fought a duel for supremacy, which eventually resulted in long strokes. Then, she captured his tongue in her mouth and sucked on it, making him moan. He reached down and cupped her ass, bringing her hips into his. She wriggled back and forth making him hard as a rock—which only caused her to press harder and move more.

"Kristen, you're killing me here."

"*Mmm.* Just making sure you're all present and accounted for."

"Oh, yeah. I'm all here, babe. It's not fair of you to take advantage of my desire for you."

"Poor baby—all that injustice. I don't know how you can *stand* it." She said as she pressed her hips in even tighter and rubbed harder against his erection.

"Now you're asking for it."

Kristen laughed. "I believe I've been asking for it all night."

"Then, it would be rude of me to disappoint a lady." He leaned down, put his shoulder into her stomach, threw her up over his shoulder, and carried her down the hall to her bedroom. There, he dumped her on the bed and pounced on her. Making her laugh.

Then they started ripping each other's clothes off— she was frantic to get to skin. When they were naked they rolled around on the bed laughing, kissing and tickling. And as they played, the heat grew until she couldn't wait any longer.

"Now, Nolan. Enough playing I want you inside, right now."

He obliged and entered her in one smooth stroke. She was ready for him and reveled in the way he filled her up. She wrapped her arms and legs around him and arched her back making him go deeper.

"Kristen, you feel like heaven. So soft and warm—and wet in just the right places."

She moaned. "And you are hard and warm, in just the right places."

He leaned down to lick her nipple and blow on it, which made it pucker—then he pulled it into his mouth and sucked hard. She lifted up pushing her breast more into his mouth. When she couldn't take it anymore he switched to the other breast and had her squirming.

He kissed his way up her chest, over her shoulder, and

up her neck to her ear where he suckled the earlobe and whispered, "Come for me."

As her body squeezed his, she screamed his name, then coaxed, "Your turn, let go and join me."

And he did. He groaned and collapsed on her, spent.

She held on tight and when he started to roll off her she said, "No wait just another few minutes. I love the feel of you pressing me into the mattress."

"You need to be able to breathe, too."

"I can breathe, kind of. It feels so good to have you on me, in me, surrounding me."

He raised up on his elbows, so he could look her in the eye. "Oh, baby, I love being a part of you."

Chapter Twenty-Four

KRISTEN WOKE TO A DELICIOUS smell coming from the kitchen—not a bad way to start the day. She put on a robe and went into the kitchen to find Nolan cooking up a feast. Eggs, bacon, hash browns, toast, orange juice, and coffee.

"Look at you, Betty Crocker," she enthused, "this is a feast fit for a king."

"Or queen, as the case may be. I was starving and figured you might be too, after all our amorous activities."

Kristen filled the mug waiting by the coffee pot. "I could eat. But first caffeine."

"Naturally."

She took her first big drink and sighed. *Heaven.* She took her cup over to the table and sat. Nolan dished up two plates of food and brought them over.

"Here you go, my sweet. Fuel for our walking adventure this morning."

She agreed. "Yes, we'll need it to wander around this morning. Any specific destination or plan of attack?"

Nolan considered. "How about we start out from here and go the direction you saw him run. Then, we'll drop down one street and zigzag until we hit Main Street and come back this way. If we have time and energy, we could go by the landing and City Park."

"Sounds like a plan."

They set out with Farley on a leash and walked along, noting how Farley acted around the people they came in contact with. He was especially friendly with children. He'd go up to them and try to give them kisses. Some children and parents loved it and some did not. He did growl at a couple of men having an argument in front of one store, but as soon as they stopped fighting he stopped rumbling. Apparently, he didn't like quarreling. Kristen had no idea he'd behave that way. Other than that, he didn't seem to act differently with any of them. Farley just walked along wagging his tail and being friendly to all.

THEY TURNED THE corner to head back up Main street when all hell broke loose. A woman was walking toward them carrying a cat and a half dozen shopping bags. The feline took one look at Farley, jumped out of the woman's arms, and took off. Nolan didn't think Farley normally paid any attention to pets, but it looked like he decided this one was playing, so he happily started chasing the cat, barking all the way.

When his leash jerked out of Kristen's hand she lost her balance as did the other woman and they both fell to the ground in a tangle of arms and legs and shopping bags. Nolan helped unravel Kristen and the tourist. He picked up the spilled bags and they all three followed the direction the animals had gone.

The cat headed toward the park, running between other shoppers and vacationers, with Farley right on her tail. They knocked down more than one person. Nolan, Kristen, and the tourist helped the people left in the wake of destruction from the wayward animals.

Since he could hear Farley howling, he knew the animals were stopped and figured the cat was safe—somewhere Farley could not get to her. They continued in the direction of the noise which, unsurprisingly, led to the park and a nice big tree the feline had climbed to get away.

The tourist turned on Kristen, hands on hips. "That dog is a menace."

"On the contrary, your cat started it." Kristen glared back. "If she hadn't taken off running, Farley wouldn't have paid any attention to your pet."

"Right, like I'm going to believe that."

Kristen took Farley's leash and told him to sit and shut up, which he did. Looking at the tourist she said, "I really don't give a rat's ass if you believe it or not."

Nolan intervened. "Now, ladies. Let's not quarrel. It was just an unfortunate…."

The tourist turned on him. "Who asked you anyway?"

Kristen spoke up. "I can handle this myself."

The tourist turned to Kristen. "Men."

"Exactly." Kristen agreed.

The tourist looked back at Nolan. "How about you really be helpful and get my cat out of the tree."

Nolan frowned, but headed toward the tree. He was just trying to help and what was this ganging up on him anyway.

He heard the woman say, "Why do men always think they have to butt in anyway? Like we are not capable of having a small disagreement."

"I know just what you mean," Kristen said.

Nolan started hauling his ass up the tree toward the damn cat. *Women.* He climbed higher toward the cat. Once he got close enough to reach it, she must have decided things were safe on the ground and nimbly went back down the tree leaving Nolan alone. Well to hell with that—another woman that wanted nothing to do with his help. Maybe he'd just stay up in the tree.

Okay, maybe he was acting like a little kid and needed to get over himself. The tourist left not saying thank you or anything about them chasing after her cat and climbing a tree, but at least she was gone and there had been no fist fight. Kristen was sitting on the grass talking to Farley about chasing cats and knocking people over.

Nolan dropped down out of the tree and sat down

on the grass next to Farley and Kristen. "I think that's sufficient for today, don't you?"

"Yeah, that's enough excitement. Thanks for trying to diffuse the situation and climbing up after the cat."

"Sure, the stupid male was happy to help—even if you didn't want my help," Nolan grumped.

KRISTEN TRIED TO hide a smile. "No worries you gave us a common bond, which diffused the anger, fear, and frustration we were feeling. It really wasn't you or what you said—just a new place to focus the tension. So, thank you for being the scape goat, so to speak."

"My pleasure," he said with a bow. "Do you want to stop by Amber's on the way for some lunch? We could tie Farley outside in the dog area. He doesn't fight with other dogs, so there shouldn't be a problem if someone else brings their dog."

Kristen considered that idea. "Sounds good. I could go for a hamburger and a stack of onion rings."

"You are my kind of woman."

They tied Farley in the dog area with a bowl of water and a dog treat. He was the only one there, so that made things easier.

Amber came over to say hi and asked if they had found the thief yet. Nolan told her no not yet, but they were still looking diligently.

The family at the next table interrupted their conversation. "Miss, do you have a children's menu?"

Amber looked over. "We have some children's selections...."

The woman interrupted, "No I mean like a children's menu that they can color and draw on, with games and stuff to keep them occupied."

"Oh, no. I don't."

"You should seriously think about getting one. All family-friendly restaurants have them you know. A menu and some crayons work wonders for keeping kids quiet and patient."

"Thanks, I'll look into it," Amber said. She turned back toward Kristen and Nolan and rolled her eyes.

Kristen mused, "You could ask Jeremy—he could design a Tsilly one for you."

"I'll give it some thought," she said and turned to go put in their orders.

As Nolan and Kristen ate they talked about Farley and how he reacted to people as they took him around the town.

"Do you think it would be worth it to take him over more toward the river to see if he can find the thief's hideout?" Kristen asked.

Nolan shook his head. "If we had something of the thief's that would give him a scent and focus him on that idea it might, but without that, I don't think Farley knows we want him to seek out anyone in particular."

"True. So do you think it's worth trying again tonight?"

Nolan lifted a shoulder. "I don't think it would hurt anything, as long as you have the time and we don't run into the cat lady."

"I'd like to get a few hours in the studio today, but other than that I'm open. The safe should be here tomorrow, I think, and the security people are coming sometime this week. So, I should be secure after that."

"Good. I don't like seeing you vulnerable and my night shifts are coming up soon."

"Maybe you'll catch the guy while you're on nights. Of course, you would need to know where to look."

Nolan grinned at her. "And that's the problem isn't it."

Kristen looked sheepish. "Yeah, I guess so, but you never know what you might see out late at night."

"Just a lot of dark, usually."

"It is a pretty quiet little town, normally. We've had a lot more tourists since the amusement park opened, and now the gallery seems to be bringing in people from the local towns. I think we need to do some advertising in some national papers or search engines or something—to bring in people from other areas."

"That's a good idea. My mom could put a link to your gallery on her page, if you've got a decent website up."

"It could use some ecommerce added to it. Right now, it's just a static website with some samples of what we have in the store. A directory of artists—that sort of thing. But since the gallery has been such a success, I can afford to pay someone to work on it and get some more features in."

"Couldn't hurt."

When they took Farley out that evening he gave no indication of anything different. Since there were also no cats to chase it wasn't a very eventful time. They went back to Kristen's with nothing new and went to bed.

Chapter Twenty-Five

THE SAFE AND THE SECURITY companies both came the next day. Two safes were delivered and installed—a larger one for the studio and one for the gallery. The studio unit would hold her gold sheets and precious gems along with any finished work she wanted stored, since the little one she brought down from the mountain only held a few finished pieces. It had been more for fire safety than protection up at her place. The gallery safe would hold the money from sales and anything else they felt should be locked up at night.

The security company started work to install a system. Kristen wasn't real excited about having to put in a code to turn on and off the alarm—she was afraid she'd not get out the door in time after keying in the number. But, once they explained she could do it from her phone, rather than the keypad, she relaxed. She didn't allow them to put a monitoring system in her living area, but they did look at the locks on the doors and windows to make sure she was as protected as possible, without the alarm arrangement.

Nolan came by while the security firm was there to talk to them about some issues he wanted addressed. One was outside flood lights that were motion-activated with a monitoring system both Kristen and the company could track. The other issue was something for the studio—which Kristen hadn't asked for. But, he convinced her to put it in, since she had sheets of metal and gems along with many work tools. She suspected his real apprehension was that she worked out there alone at night. Fine. She could deal with his concern for her. If it helped him not to worry she was willing to let them put it in, although she knew she could handle herself.

Kristen did feel more protected with the alarm systems in place. She wasn't used to living in town and having so many people around, so having some security was an added precaution. Nolan started his night rotation the following week, so she wouldn't have him around. She wasn't worried about safety without him, but she was wondering if she'd be lonely. She'd just have to get over it, because she was still planning to go back up the mountain once the fire was out. Wasn't she?

Kristen decided to have a late lunch at Amber's on the last day of the week. The security people would be finishing up and she was glad—she was getting tired of all the hub-bub. She went into the mostly empty restaurant and sat at a table near the back. Some alone time was what she needed. She ordered her lunch and was looking at her website on her phone when someone cleared his throat next to her. Standing next to her was the person they thought was the thief.

He asked, "Can I sit?" and motioned to the seat across from her with a very large hunting knife.

Kristen gulped and nodded. She looked around the restaurant and didn't see anyone.

He sat down and set the knife on the table. Then he smiled shyly at her. "I'm Ted. I saw you at your store."

"I'm Kristen and I saw you too." She looked closely at him. He really didn't look very old—he might even be a teenager, but he'd clearly spent a lot of time outdoors, which gave him a weathered look.

"You remind me of someone a long time ago, when I was just a baby."

"Oh? Like your mother."

Ted jumped like he'd been slapped. "Shhh don't say that word, it's a bad word. Pa doesn't like it when I say that word."

Kristen raised her eyebrows, but said, "Is your Pa with you?"

Ted shook his head. "No, he died four summers ago. I had to bury him."

"Oh, sorry. Do you live with anyone else?"

"No just me and Pa—and then just me."

"Did you live up in the mountains? Before the fire?"

"Yeah, me and Pa have a cabin up there, but I had to leave when the fire came."

Kristen nodded. "Yes, so did I. Did you live there a long time?"

"Yeah, since I was little."

"So Ted, did you take some things from my store?"

"Yes, I traded my rocks for a blanket and some candles and flower smelling soap and the secret and this green paper that you give people for things." Ted reached in his pocket and put a fist full of money on the table.

Kristen could tell most of the three hundred dollars he'd taken was right there in the pile on the table. Kristen nodded at the money. "You haven't used very much of that money."

Ted asked, "Money? Is that the green paper's name?"

"Yes, it's used to buy things from people rather than just taking it."

"I saw people giving it to that other lady in your store. And I saw people giving it to the lady for food here."

"So, you've not seen it before?" Kristen asked, again looking around the restaurant for anyone. What was taking her food so long?

Ted shook his head. "Oh, no. I've never been out of our homestead. I didn't know there were people just down the mountain from it. We had some people walking around a time or two up by our house. Pa would borrow some things from them sometimes. Like this knife. I was just going to take it hunting when the fire came and I had to run away from the house. I had to leave everything else—even the secret."

"What secret, Ted?"

"Oh, this secret," he said as he dug a small wooden cross out of his pocket. "It's not the real secret—that one is buried up at the cabin. I hope the fire didn't burn it. It wasn't made of wood, but metal like the knife—only yellow."

"Gold?"

"Maybe, but since I didn't have the real one and the angel said to keep it with me always—but never show it to Pa—I made this one to look like it."

"Can I see it, Ted?"

"Yes, because you aren't Pa. See, I had to put the design in. The secret I got from your store didn't have it."

Kristen picked it up and saw Theodore Beaumont etched in the cross. Just then Ben and Nolan came up to the table in full uniform with the snap on their guns off, ready for use.

"Mind if we sit?"

Ted smiled at Nolan, "Sit. You are Kristen's friend." Then he looked at Ben, "I've seen you too, sit."

Nolan slid in next to Kristen and Ben sat next to Ted. Ted showed no signs of nervousness being surrounded by police, even though he'd just admitted to her that he'd taken those things from her store. Kristen thought this was the strangest lunch ever, but she introduced Ted to the officers.

Nolan said, "So Ted, what brings you to be sitting here with Kristen?"

"She talked to me another day and I was scared to talk to people, so I ran away. But then I wanted to talk to someone real bad, so when I saw her come in, I came in too. I've seen people sitting and talking in here before. So, I thought it would be okay. Oh, and I have some new rocks for her."

"Why the knife?"

"The knife? I always carry it. Especially since the fire. It was the only thing I had when the fire came and I had to run away."

"So you don't want to hurt someone with it?"

"No, that would be bad. A knife is for hunting and fishing and cutting sticks and things like that. Never people!"

"How old are you Ted?"

"Old? What do you mean?"

Kristen said, "His Pa died four years ago. How many summers did you live with your Pa in the mountains?"

"I don't really know. Since I was a little kid. Maybe eight or ten summers?"

Kristen held out the cross. "Take a look at this. It's the one from my shop only Ted decorated it to match the one that's buried up at his house."

Nolan and Ben looked at the cross and then exchanged

a look. Nolan asked, "Would you mind if I took the knife for a minute, Ted?"

"You can take it, but I need it back before I leave."

Nolan took the knife and got up from the booth.

Kristen looked at Ted. "Ted, earlier you said you traded rocks for the things you took from the store. What did you mean?"

"My rocks. I saw there were lots of pretty things in your store so I left some of my rocks."

Kristen's mouth dropped open. "Are you talking about the sculptures?"

"I don't know what a sculpture is, but I have more in my bag that I can show you."

Ben said, "Can I get those out for you? I put your bag on the floor when I sat down."

"Sure."

Ben picked up the bag he'd put in the aisle and opened it. He pulled out a few rock sculptures and put them on the table. One was an eagle with wings extended ready to take flight. Another was a perfect reproduction of one of the mountains. Another was of a mother bear and her cubs.

"You sculpted those?"

"I don't know what sculpted means, but I took a big rock and kinda carved out the extra to make what I wanted. I thought maybe you could trade them for money in your store. Can you trade them for money?"

"Yes, I did sell or trade some of the others you left for money. In fact, I need to give you a bit more money since they sold for more than you took. They are very beautiful."

"Thanks, I like to figure out how to take a big rock and make it into something else."

"Well, you do a good job."

Nolan came back to the table. "Ted, I need to take you to the police station and ask you a few more questions. We are going to need you to spend a couple of days there."

"But, what about my camp? Do you have somewhere for me to sleep? I didn't bring anything else with me."

"I can send someone to go get your things if you tell us where they are. We do have a nice room you can sleep in and we'll need to have a CPS person talk with you since you might be a minor."

"I don't know any CPS people, do I?"

"No, but here comes one now. She's a nice lady and she can help you."

"Can't Kristen be my person? Are you mad at me for taking the things from other stores? I can trade the other stores my rocks? Or Kristen says she needs to give me more money for the rocks I left her—I could give that to those people. I was kind of afraid I was making people mad by taking their things, but I didn't know what else to do."

"It's alright Ted, we just need you to come with us. Kristen has to go back to her house to feed her dog," Nolan said.

"Oh, I'm sorry I made him sick, so I could go in your store Kristen. But, I ate those mushrooms once and they just made me sleepy, so I knew he would be okay. I'll come with you Nolan. Can I talk to you again, Kristen, if you aren't too mad at me?"

"I forgive you, Ted. I'll come by and see you tomorrow."

Several hours later, when Nolan finally showed up at Kristen's, she was bursting with curiosity about what had happened with Ted. He explained that Ted thought the jail was the most comfortable place he had ever been. He had been amazed at the toilet and how it worked and was happy to have a bed not on the floor. He was also surprised that they were going to bring him food that he didn't have to hunt for himself. He was pretty excited to have all that extravagance.

Kristen laughed, but felt sad for the boy too. Imagine thinking a jail cell was the lap of luxury.

They had asked him a few questions and the CPS person agreed with them—they didn't believe he had any idea what he was doing was wrong. The main thing they asked him about was his past. They wanted to see if they could find his family. If he had any. They felt the cross and some of the things he'd said indicated his father might have abducted him. They were going to start with the name he had engraved on the cross.

After Nolan finished his explanation of what had happened with Ted, he stood and drew Kristen to her feet before wrapping his arms around her. "I was so terrified when I got the call from dispatch, that you were in that restaurant at the table with Ted, and that the big hunting knife was between you on the table. I didn't know if I would get there and find you being held hostage."

"But, he wasn't dangerous."

Nolan smiled. "We know that now, but at the time of the call we didn't."

"No, and when he first sat down and laid that knife on the table I was pretty freaked out too. But it became obvious pretty quickly that he wasn't there to harm me. I was damn glad to see you and Ben come in the door, though."

"Well, I was damn glad to see you sitting there having a chat. I could finally breathe again." Nolan took her face in his hands and kissed her like he was starving for her. He devoured her and claimed her and made her feel like she was air for him at that moment. She felt her entire body yearn for him. She needed him, too—nearly like an addiction. It was heady and powerful and she'd never felt anything like it before. She just knew this was right.

"Well, let's go celebrate our mutual damn gladness. I want to reward my hero for coming to my rescue."

Chapter Twenty-Six

NOLAN WOKE WITH A JERK. The nightmare. But this time it wasn't his sister being raped and murdered, it was Kristen. He couldn't do this anymore—he couldn't be with her, it was too big of a risk. He had to get out of her bed, her house, her life. He slowly untangled himself from her arms, grabbed his clothes, and went to the bathroom to get dressed.

When he came out, Kristen sat up looking adorably rumpled. "Are you leaving? I thought we were spending the day together."

"Yes, I'm leaving and no, we're not spending the day together. In fact, I think we should stop seeing each other."

"What? Stop seeing each other? What do you mean by that?"

He steeled himself against the hurt in her eyes. "I don't

think we should be together like this anymore. It's not good, it's too much." He got his weapon from her dresser and strapped it on.

"Too much of what? Not good how? What in the hell are you talking about?"

"I can't explain it. I just can't be with you. Hearing you were trapped at Amber's with Ted—it was just too much." Nolan started out the door.

When he stopped at the door to put his shoes on Kristen was right behind him tying the sash on her robe. "Are you running away from this because of Ted? He's just a kid, he was never any real danger."

"Yes, but that doesn't mean there's no real danger out there."

"Oh, I get it. Like your sister. You're afraid something like that will happen again, so you're not going to get involved with someone. Well, that's just too damn bad. You are already involved."

"Not anymore, and what about my sister?"

"Your mother told me all about it."

"Great, just great. Say what you will, but I'm out of here." He jerked the door open and raced down the steps like the hounds of hell were after him, when in reality, it was the fear of a beautiful woman.

Kristen watched in shock as Nolan left. *Fine. Be a chicken shit.* She didn't care. *Stupid man. Who needs one anyway? I've wasted enough time on him.* But now what? She'd planned to spend the day with him and had made arrangements to do just that. She could reorder her whole schedule to be with him and he just ran out on her. And to think she'd even planned to miss the gem show in Idaho just to spend more time with him. Putting him ahead of her career? Not a very smart move. Of course, she could always shop for her gems online, but it wasn't the same as holding the cabs in her hand. *Damn him.* Well, she refused to cry over him.

I'll just pack up my truck and go to the gem show. It's not too late.

She firmly put Nolan out of her mind, let Farley out, and grabbed the phone to call and see if she could get her truck on the barge this afternoon. No time to get her camping gear together, she would have to find motels that were dog-friendly. If she got moving quick enough she could stop by the small gem show in Walla Walla before driving on to Boise.

For the rest of the morning she moved like a whirlwind making arrangements and packing. She called Mary Ann and Barbara to let them know she'd be gone about a week. She stopped by the jail to tell Ted she was not going to be around for a while. He did look happy in his cell. She made it to the landing just in time to meet the barge returning downlake from Stehekin. She was not running away, she was just doing her job—Nolan had nothing to do with it. At least that's what she kept telling herself.

NOLAN SPENT THE DAY at his house catching up on chores, cleaning, doing laundry, trying to get his mind off Kristen. He'd been an ass—he knew that—but he just couldn't keep the nightmare at bay. It would destroy him to lose her like that. He needed to have a talk with his mother about her telling Kristen about his sister, but not today. Today he needed to get his head on straight—and good hard work was the way to do that. But the house was clean and the laundry was done and it was barely noon. Now what?

Wood chopping! There was a pile of it in the back of the yard where a tree or two had been sawn into foot-long cylinders that needed to be split. Not that he would need it soon, since there was a stack of it by the back door that might last the full winter—but since it was his first year here, he had no idea, so might as well work on it.

Nolan could barely move when he finally stopped for dinner. Who knew chopping wood was such hard work? He dragged himself into the kitchen, wolfed down a sandwich, and headed for the shower where he turned the water on as hot as he could stand. His muscles were screaming and the heat would help some. He downed a hand full of ibuprofen and hauled himself to bed. It was hours before sundown, but he felt himself being pulled into sleep and was glad for hard work that had tired him out.

The next morning, he hobbled into work, still sore after another boiling shower and handful of pain killers. He decided he might have over done the wood splitting just a bit.

Chief MacGregor signaled him into his office before he could even grab some coffee.

"You'll never guess who young Ted is. He's a boy who was kidnapped by his father fourteen years ago, when he was three. His mother was the daughter of Theodore Beaumont the third, the railroad tycoon. Ted is named after his grandfather although his last name is Jordan. His mom did a lot of work to try to find him—TV appearances, news articles, rewards, anything she could think of."

"I knew that cross seemed familiar, I must have seen something on it."

"Every police department in America has him listed as a missing person."

"We've contacted his mother and she's on her way here. You'll need to make sure Kristen and the other store owners are willing to not press charges before we can release him."

Nolan stifled a groan. Kristen, he'd been an ass to the woman and now he needed to contact her. "Do you want me to contact them or one of the other officers?"

"You made the arrest, you make the contacts. Ben's off

today and I'm thinking the mother is going to be here as quick as she can get here, maybe even today."

"But she can't get here that fast."

"Private jets and plenty of money can work wonders. Get on it."

Nolan walked out of the office and straight to his cruiser. He decided to contact all the other store owners first and leave Kristen for last. Chicken? Yes. Yes, he was.

A few hours later he admitted he couldn't put it off any longer. He'd connected with all the store owners, and none of them wanted to press charges, but they did give him a list of compensation they wanted in return. Now all he had left was Kristen—time to face the music. He drove up to her house and parked in the street. The gallery was still open so he went inside.

"Hi, Nolan," Tim Jefferson called out.

"Hi, Tim. Is Kristen around?"

"No, I haven't seen her today."

"Oh, have you been to the studio?"

"No, feel free to go on back, but I didn't see Farley this afternoon, either."

"Thanks," he said. He started to have a very bad feeling about all this. He went back to the studio and she wasn't there and her truck was gone—along with the bowls she kept in the yard for Farley. Maybe she'd gone up the mountain.

He ran out to his cruiser and started up to where he had first met her, the road was no longer closed from the fire, since it had moved deeper into the mountains and farther away from the town. It was a steep, dangerous road so it took him over an hour to reach her place and that was with him driving a little faster than he should have. When he arrived at the house it looked like the firefighters were still using it as a base camp. Her truck was nowhere to be seen.

He got out and went up to the door. Trey answered.

"Hi, Nolan. What's up?"

"Just wondering if Kristen had been up here today."

"Nope, not that I know of. Don't you know where she is? I thought you guys were tight."

"I kind of blew it this morning, but I need to ask her about an official matter."

"Oh, well, I would guess either Mary Ann or Barbara would know where she is. Did you ask them?"

"No, but I will. Thanks. How's the fire?"

"Still burning—fortunately not toward town. We're just doing what we can and hoping for an early snowfall."

"Well, I gotta get going. Take care."

Nolan got in his car and headed back down the mountain. Where was she? He supposed he was going to have to suck it up and ask someone. He so didn't want to have to do that, but he really had no choice. Ted's mother could be there any minute and Kristen was the last one affected by him. She'd been kind toward Ted and hadn't mentioned pressing charges, but he couldn't just guess at her reaction—he had to know for sure.

When he got back to town his shift was about over so he took the cruiser to the station.

A very well-dressed woman and her entourage had taken over the office—clearly the mother had arrived. Darn. She seemed to be very upset, so he figured he was in trouble for taking so long.

The chief waved Nolan into his office. "Close the door, Nolan."

"Chief, I've contacted everyone, but Kristen. I haven't found her yet."

"Yeah, yeah. We have bigger problems than that. Ted refuses to see his mother. He kind of freaked out when we mentioned her. And since then he won't talk to me. I want you to go back and see if you can find out what's going on."

"Okay."

"He seems to trust you—just don't mention the word mother, it seems to make him crazy."

Nolan walked into the cell area. "Hey, Ted."

"Hi, Nolan."

"Do you mind if I come in and sit with you?"

"That would be nice."

Nolan unlocked the door and went into the cell. "So, how's it going?"

"Kinda weird, Nolan. Chief MacGregor came in here talking about an m-word and scared me."

"An m-word?"

"Yes, it's a very bad word and my pa used to get really mad at me if I said it and punish me a lot. So, I don't say it and it scares me to hear other people say it."

"I see, but your pa is dead now so he can't punish you."

Ted looked back and forth in a furtive manner. "But, what if someone else hears it and gets mad at me?"

"I don't think that's going to happen. Do you want to try?"

"Can you say it first? While I hold my hands over my ears, so I can't hear it."

"Sure." Ted put his hands over his ears and Nolan said, "Mother."

Ted looked all around again.

Nolan said, "Now put your hands over your ears and you say it."

Ted put his hand over his ears and whispered, "Mother." He flinched and looked around. Then he said it a little louder, "Mother." He took his hands off his ears and said it one more time. "Mother."

"Good for you, Ted. Now, do you know what a mother is?"

"No, just that it's a bad word."

Nolan smiled warmly. "No, Ted, A mother is the female of a pa. She's the one who birthed you."

"Oh, is that all? I've seen lots of mother animals then, giving birth to their babies."

"Exactly." Nolan nodded. "Nothing bad at all. Now, it looks like your pa took you and hid you from your mother and her family when you were just a little guy."

Ted frowned. "That sounds kind of mean."

"Yeah it does, but we don't know why he did it. Your mother has been looking for you for fourteen years. We contacted her to let her know you had been found and she would very much like to talk to you."

"I guess that would be okay. Does she look nice or mean?"

"Very nice, Ted. I think you'll like her."

"Can you stay in here with me while I talk to her?"

"I can do that. I'll be right back." Nolan locked the cell and went to get Ted's mother.

He explained the situation to the chief, who then explained it to Ted's mother, Lenore, who burst into tears for her poor baby. Nolan thought about how messed up the situation was and decided he needed to call his own mother. And he needed to talk to Kristen—and not just about Ted.

Nolan cleared his throat. "Ma'am your son is waiting to talk to you."

"Oh, right. Let me just wash these tears off and we'll go talk to him."

Nolan took her back to the cell area and when Ted looked up and saw his mother he whispered in awe, "The angel."

"What did you say, Ted?"

"The angel. You brought me the angel."

"This is your mother, Ted."

"My mother is the angel? The angel loved me and was always nice to me. I cried when I didn't see her anymore."

Lenore said, "I do love you, Teddy, and I cried when I didn't see you anymore, too."

Nolan unlocked the cell and let Lenore in to see her

son. He stayed in the cell area so he could see them, but let them have some privacy.

After they talked for a while, Lenore left the cell and came over to Nolan.

"He said he wants to stay in his room tonight. He seems to feel safe in there, so I'm going to go check into the hotel and come back in the morning. Chief MacGregor mentioned you were talking with the store owners Ted stole things from. I'm happy to pay any restitution needed."

"All of the store owners are fine with that. There is just one I haven't tracked down yet. I don't think she will feel any differently, but we should probably keep him until I can find her."

"I understand. I'll just say good bye to Ted and come back in the morning."

"Thanks for being understanding."

"Ted thinks highly of you and says you've been nice to him. Thank you for finding my son and giving him back to me."

Nolan nodded and waited while they said goodbye. Then, he said goodnight to Ted, relocked the cell, and headed toward the front, He needed to find Kristen. His shift was over so he clocked out and let the chief know he would be contacting Kristen. He climbed in his car and decided if anyone knew where Kristen was, it would be Barbara. So, he drove by her shop, but it looked closed down. He turned his car toward their home and hoped Kristen was with them.

He didn't see Kristen's truck, so he went and knocked

on the door. Chris answered looking frazzled. "Nolan, come on in."

He heard Barbara call out. "Chris, who is it? Whoever it is tell them to go away. It's dinner time and the baby is hungry and my feet are too swollen to cook and you have to dooooo something."

Good grief, what was going on here? He started backing toward the door and Chris grabbed onto him like he was his savior. "Nolan, you distract her while I get her some food—so she doesn't explode."

Chris yanked him toward the family room where Barbara was sitting with her feet propped up and three fans blowing on her. She had a gigantic glass of water next to her and washcloths covered her neck, both wrists, both ankles, and her eyes. A bucket of ice water was next to her where more cloths floated. Chris pushed him into the room and fled.

"Barbara? It's me, Nolan."

Not moving an inch, she said, "Hi, Nolan. Did you bring food?"

"Um, no, but Chris is on that. Are you feeling okay?"

"No, I'm not. I feel like I'm in a furnace roasting to death. Why is it so damn hot and what's taking Chris so long to get me some food?"

"I think it's hot because it's summer and I'm sure Chris will be here in a minute. So, I need to find Kristen. Do you know where she is?"

"Yes, at the gem show in Idaho—or no, she may still

be in Walla Walla and going on to Idaho tomorrow or maybe the next day."

"Gem show?"

"Yes, didn't she tell you about it? She goes every year, although I didn't think she was planning to go this year. I guess she changed her mind. She was running out of stones to set, so she probably decided to get after it and go. Gotta keep her customers happy. What is taking Chris so long?"

"So, how long will she be gone?"

"Oh, about a week. The gem shows are normally on the weekends—what day is it anyway? This pregnancy has made me a little confused." She sighed.

"Saturday."

"Then she is at the Walla Walla one today and tomorrow and then she'll drive over to Idaho for next weekend, so I guess it'll be a little longer than a week. Chris where the hell are you, the baby is starving!" She yelled so loud Nolan practically dove for cover and drew his weapon.

"Right here, sweetheart," he said as he rolled his eyes at Nolan.

"Okay, well, I'll let you two have dinner."

Chris set his tray down next to the ice water and followed him, calling over his shoulder, "I'll just let Nolan out and be right back."

Barbara nodded as she shoveled food into her mouth.

"Chris, for Pete's sake, go buy a damn air conditioner or three. And get your sister to have food ready and on hand at all times. Planning man, you need planning. How far along is she anyway?"

"Just a few months. This baby is going to be the death of me."

"Well, get your act together, dude, and get some ready-made food in this house and air conditioning."

"But, we might only have a few more days of this heat."

"In a few days you could be murdered by your wife and then I would have to arrest her and make sure she has food and air conditioning in the jail cell."

"Chris!" Barbara yelled.

"Just go buy a damn air conditioner or I might have to shoot you myself." He jogged down the sidewalk to his car, shaking his head at Chris. How could he be married to her for ten years and still not have a clue? He'd heard rumors that they had gone through some tough times recently in their marriage, but they seemed fine now. Things would go even better if Chris started using his head a bit more.

Nolan got in the car and pulled out his cell phone. He needed to call Kristen and he wasn't putting it off another minute. He found her name and pushed send, but the phone just rang. When he got voicemail, he said, "Kristen? Hi, it's Nolan. We found Ted's mother and she wants to make restitution for anything he's done. It turns out Ted was kidnapped by his father fourteen years ago. Anyway, we need to make sure you are okay with accepting restitution and not pressing charges. You can also press charges if you want. We just have to know your decision to decide if we keep him incarcerated. Please call me back, or calling dispatch would be fine too."

He hung up. He'd wanted to say something personal, but he really didn't know what. He needed to see her face to face and that wasn't going to happen for over a week. What a dumbass he'd been. The woman was amazing and he was a chicken shit to push her away rather than taking a chance. He hoped she would call him back, but he wouldn't be surprised if she called dispatch instead.

Chapter Twenty-Seven

KRISTEN WANDERED THROUGH the gem show in Walla Walla. There were some nice things displayed, but she had trouble focusing on what she needed. She knew she had to get it together. When she got in town the previous night, she'd sent all her major clients an email telling them she would be attending some shows and asking if any of them had specific desires for stones. Then, she'd crashed. Getting dumped, packing, and driving for four hours while crying most of the way had a tendency to wear a person out.

When she'd woken up that morning, she had several emails with lists of what her clients wanted. She'd spent some time during breakfast making a consolidated list including what she wanted to pick up for stock. She was nearly out of the blue stones for the jewelry she had in

Barbara's wedding shop. She also needed more of the tiny chips for the Tsilly and Kalar charms she sold like hotcakes, due to the popularity of the game and now the amusement park.

She also wanted to get some cabs for her more unique jewelry—she needed some for her art gallery. And the galleries in Leavenworth and Wenatchee were both asking for more as soon as possible. She'd been spending too much time with that man and had fallen behind on her work.

Well no more of that. I'm going to focus on my work, not Nolan the rat.

She stopped at a table and looked at her list. There was a couple nice cabs that might work. She took some pictures with her phone and texted them to the clients she was thinking of, to see if they liked them. She spent the next hour texting back and forth between her clients and purchasing some nice stones. Her phone started showing low power, so she texted them all one last time and told them she would have a fully charged battery for the next day. She turned off her phone to save the tiny bit of power she had left—just in case she needed it—before she could get to a charger or the power bank in her luggage. She sighed. Doesn't do a lot of good in the luggage. *I'll have it more together tomorrow.*

She spent a little more time looking at the tables until she got too hungry to stay and went off to her hotel, grabbing a salad, chicken sandwich, and bottle of wine on the way back.

While her phone charged, she ate her food and worked on the lists of cabochons she needed and what she'd seen at the show to fill it. It was a long list and she knew there was no way she would be able to get everything at the Walla Walla show, so she would be driving into Idaho for the four-day event in Boise. She wanted to look around for some new stones while she was there too—maybe pick up some cabs she'd never used before. That would be fun.

She took Farley out for a walk and looked around the town. When she got back to the hotel she saw her phone was fully charged. She noticed two voice messages and two missed calls. One of the missed calls was from Nolan. Well, that was interesting. Did she want to even hear what he had to say? Of course, she did, but she also wanted to delete it and stay in a snit. She wouldn't erase it, but the idea of it made her smile evilly. It would serve him right, but she wasn't a person to cut her nose off to spite her face. So, she pushed the voicemail number to listen.

The first message was from Shelly with a few more requests. She was thinking about a matching necklace set for herself and her two granddaughters. And then she thought that if she did a set for the kids, the adult women in the family would want their own jewelry, too. Kristen laughed at Shelly's message and then wrote down her requests on the ever-growing list.

The second message was from Nolan and it was all business. Well, fine. Be that way! He couldn't say one word to her about *them*, rat fink that he is. She decided to call dispatch and let them know she was happy to let Ted go, she didn't want to press charges, and the amount she had sold his sculptures for, more than made up for what he had taken from the store, and the new ones he'd given her would sell easily. She was glad they had found his family and that he was not alone in the world.

A few days later Kristen answered her cell. "Hi, sis. How's it going?"

"Great," Barbara answered. "Are you in Boise?"

"Yep, it's a great show. I'm picking up lots of new stones. But one of the vendors keeps flirting with me, trying to talk me into going to his home to see other stones he has."

"What? Sounds kinda like come look at my etchings. Does he live in Boise?"

"Exactly. And no, he doesn't live in Boise. Crazy man."

"Well, just be careful. There are a lot of weird people in the world."

"Don't worry, I'm not going to go off with some strange guy." Kristen laughed.

"So, the reason I called. I was thinking about that pretty red stone you have that is that long skinny teardrop shape."

"Yes, the cuprite from Mexico."

"Can you look and see if there is any of that in the show? I'd kind of like some of that for myself."

"Okay, will do. Any particular size or shape you're looking for?"

Barbara sighed. "Not really. I just like it and think I should have you make me something to commemorate the baby."

"Aww, that's a nice idea. I'll be in touch when I find some."

"Cool. Thanks. Have fun—see you in a few days."

A FEW DAYS later Kristen called Barbara's cell phone, but it went to voice mail. "Hey sis, I decided to go to the Denver show. I'm going to meet up with Shelly to do some more stone shopping and show her what I have for her so far. I did find one cuprite in Boise, but the vendor, Sam, said there's a slab at the shop in Alamosa that can be made into custom cabs for me. So, after the Denver show, I'm going to go look. I won't be back for another week or ten days. Take care of yourself. I'll be in touch"

Chapter Twenty-Eight

NOLAN WENT INTO KRISTEN'S gallery and looked around. He didn't see her anywhere; she should be back this week. He had a few days off and he was going to fix this thing with Kristen—he missed her and they were good together.

Mary Ann saw him. She was on the phone, but excused herself from the conversation for a moment. She looked slightly apprehensive.

"Are you looking for Kristen?"

He nodded.

"She's not going to be back for at least another week. I can't talk now and this call is going to take a while, but she left a message with Barbara. Go on over there and she can fill you in."

"Thanks," he said and headed for the exit to walk next door to Barbara's business.

He walked inside and Christa came out from the back. She was startled to see him and then looked at him sympathetically. He wondered what was going on—Christa was not good at hiding her feelings, so he knew something was up.

"Hi, Nolan. Barbara's upstairs, go on up." She smiled brightly at him, a little too brightly.

He went up the stairs to the top floor where Barbara's office was and knocked on the open door frame before stepping into her office-slash-studio. Barbara looked up from the design she was working on and immediately set her pencil down. That wasn't a good sign, since Barbara had a one-track mind and never—to his knowledge anyway—stopped mid-work.

"Nolan, come in," she said as she stood and walked toward him. "Can I get you something to drink? Water? Coffee? Scotch?"

Nolan raised his eyebrows. "Scotch? Now?"

"You might need it," she muttered under her breath. Then she plastered a big smile on her face and spoke up. "What can I do for you?"

"You can tell me where Kristen is. I thought she was coming home this week."

"Well, she's looking for some specific stones, so she went on to the gem show in Denver, this weekend…."

"Mary Ann said she was going to be gone at least another week, maybe longer. It's only a two-day drive."

"Right…" Barbara cleared her throat. "After the show in Denver she's going down to Alamosa. There's a gem cutter down there that has more of a particular stone and will make some custom cabs for her."

"That's very generous."

"Right," Barbara said with a snort.

"Is there more to this story you aren't telling me?"

Barbara looked chagrined. She said quietly, "I don't know for sure, but...."

"Go on."

"Well, some gem cutter was hitting on her, he invited her to his house. She said she wasn't interested, but now she's going to a shop in Alamosa with some guy named Sam. I don't know if it's the same guy...."

Nolan felt his stomach drop to his feet, but kept a stoic expression on his face. He was a cop after all and could hide his emotions with the best of them. "I see. Well, we won't know what's going on until she gets back. Thanks." He walked quickly out of the shop, down the stairs, and out the door. He got into his car, hit his steering wheel with his fist, and swore.

He was too late and it was all his fault—he was going to lose her. But it had only been a few days and she was going off with some other guy. Not that he could blame *Sam* for hitting on her, she was a beautiful woman. How could any man resist her? But still *he* hadn't gone out and found a new girl. Although he hadn't been dumped and this Sam had probably seen her in a vulnerable state. Yes, it was all his fault. He knew he'd been a dumbass.

He got home and couldn't settle. He wasn't interested in eating or watching TV and he sure as hell couldn't read. Didn't want to work in the yard or on his car, and he figured he had enough wood chopped for the winter. He looked toward the building he had his glass making supplies in. No, probably not a good idea in his present state of mind. He'd burn the place down—or maybe burn himself.

He turned away and went into his bedroom. Maybe he should go for a jog. He looked at his running shoes and out the window toward the shed. He'd always been able to get lost in glass—he could turn his mind off and revel in the art of it. Maybe.

He grabbed a bottle of water and went out to the workroom. As he walked into the heat, he knew he could forget—for a while—in this place. He looked at the sculpture drawings he'd started before Kristen had been robbed. It wasn't bad, but it was too soft, too dreamy. It needed more. An idea started to form in his head.

Chapter Twenty-Nine

KRISTEN WAS GLAD TO BE home. She'd had a very successful trip and she was excited to get to work on the pieces she had in her head. But God, she was ready for her own house and her own bed and shower. Being with so many people had drained her. She'd enjoyed her time away with clients and other jewelry professionals, but she was ready for her friends and family and some peace and quiet. She might even track Nolan down and force him to talk about why he'd broken up with her. The last few weeks had given her perspective, and she knew something had triggered his shut down. It wasn't like him at all, and he was at least going to explain himself. Even if they didn't get back together she wanted answers and closure.

She pulled her car into the drive and around to the back. She needed to unload her purchases into her studio and take her suitcase into the house, but first she wanted to check in with Mary Ann, and she should probably also go over to see her sister and find out how the pregnancy was going. She'd talked to Barbara occasionally, but the conversations had been a little stilted and Barbara had cut them short with excuses. Kristen was worried something was wrong, but when she asked, Barbara had said everything was fine.

Kristen went into the gallery in search of Mary Ann. She found her restocking the fancy soaps. She also noticed some leatherwork items that had not been there before. Interesting.

"Hi, Mary Ann. I'm back."

"Oh, Kristen, it's great to see you. We missed you."

"God, I missed you and this place, too. The shopping trip was great, but I am glad to be home. I've got so many new cabs for us to work on—it's going to be really fun."

Mary Ann laughed. "Goody, we're running low on jewelry. We've had lots of sales while you were gone. I haven't had much time to work on anything other than the Tsilly charms—people at the amusement park have kept us cleaned out."

"Do we need more help?"

"Probably not, but we can talk about it and see. Now that you're back it will make a difference."

"So, where did the leather work come from?"

Mary Ann looked over toward the leather display. "The Jeffersons—Hank and Mike both do it and even Alyssa, when she's not too busy at the amusement park and flirting with boys. Ellen finally talked Hank into putting some of his work in here and Mike followed suit. It's beautiful."

"It is. They're very talented." Kristen picked up one of the hand-tooled boxes and examined it. "What a great jewelry box this would make."

"That's what I thought. And look at the purses and wallets. Hank does cowboy boots, too, but that would take up too much room with all the different sizes."

"True. This is a great addition, but we don't want to become a leather store, and I don't imagine Hank and Mike have that much time to work on things anyway, with running the cattle ranch and Mike being in college."

"So, what else happened while I was away? How is the fire? I kept tabs on it from the Chelan County Emergency Management Facebook page, but you've got an inside scoop, providing you're still seeing the hottie firefighter."

Mary Ann blushed. "Yes, I'm still seeing Trey. They've got the fire contained, as long as we don't have any more lightning strikes to start other spots burning. For the most part, they are just waiting for the first snowfall to really put it out. Your house is pretty safe. They are still using it as a base of operations, but you can move back if you want to."

"Actually, I'm not sure I want to. I kind of enjoy living in town."

"Really? That would be awesome. I love you being here."

"I also plan to talk to Nolan."

Mary Ann gaped at her. "But I thought…."

"Thought what?"

Barbara burst in the door right then and interrupted. "You're back, it's about time. I thought this baby was going to be born before you finally got here." Mary Ann shook her head and went back to work.

"That's silly—you aren't due for months and I was only gone two and a half weeks."

"Almost three and it seemed like forever," Barbara whined.

"Is that pregnancy hormones talking?"

"No. Maybe. You've never gone on a buying trip that long. And just who is this Sam person? I thought you weren't going to hook up with him."

"Him who?"

"The gem cutter that was flirting with you in Walla Walla and wanting you to come to his shop. Sam from Alamosa."

"The gem cutter in Walla Walla was named Matthew and he lives in Portland. Sam who lives in Alamosa is a female, *Samantha*."

Kristen watched as all the blood drained from her sister's face. "Oh, my God."

"What's wrong Barbara? Here sit down."

"Oh, Kristen, I'm so sorry. I thought you were with a guy in Alamosa. Nolan came in looking for you and I told him you were with a guy, and he was so hurt. He tried not to show it, but I could see it."

"Well, that does explain why I got messages from him at first, but not recently."

"Do you want to be with him? Do you think you can fix it?" Barbara asked.

"Well, I definitely want to talk to him. If we can get back together great, but if not I at least want some closure. He just walked out one day and I have no real idea why."

Barbara hugged her. "I hope it works out. You can tell him I was confused. I'm going back to the shop—Chris bought me an air conditioner for my office, so I never leave, except to go home, because he also bought two more for the house. He's the best."

Kristen walked out to her car amazed that Barbara would think she would hook up with a stranger just a few days after she'd been with Nolan. Now that she thought about it, Mary Ann had acted a little odd too. What was wrong with all of them? She wasn't a rebound kind of girl. Sure, she'd had a few relationships over the years, but never back to back. Silly people. They had known her all her life, but it was clear they didn't understand her very well—even her own sister.

So, Nolan probably thought the same, but he had broken it off. Should she go after him anyway? She'd missed him while she was gone. Did she really want to just let the best guy she'd ever been with get away, over a misunderstanding? No, probably not. She should at least talk to him and see if they could work out their differences.

She called his cell phone, but it went straight to voice mail. So, she called dispatch—the non-emergency line—to see if he was on duty. Of course, she would pretend to be calling about Ted. She was curious about the boy, so it wouldn't be a lie.

"Chedwick police and fire. Is this an emergency?"

"No, Michelle. This is Kristen."

"Hi, Kristen. Are you back from Denver? Did you get me some malachite cabs for earrings? I love the pendant and bracelet so much, but I need some earrings, too."

Kristen laughed. "Yes, I'm back from Denver and I got three sets of malachite cabs for earrings. You'll have to come by and tell me which ones you want. I assume you want the same design as the others."

"Oh, goody. I'm off Monday. Will that work?"

"That would be perfect. It will take me a few days to get everything sorted and ready. I was wondering if I needed to come in to do anything formal about Ted. How did everything work out?"

"Oh, I don't know if anything formal is needed. Nolan would be the one to ask. He's off today and tomorrow—I guess you haven't talked to him since you went to Denver."

"No, I was having some cell issues and then was busy with clients and gem cutters. Samantha from Alamosa had a really nice slab of cuprite, so I went down and had her cut me some custom cabs. So, I didn't have time to chat with him."

"Alamosa? Samantha? A female? Oh, um, never mind. Hey, I've got another call—I better go. You can probably find Nolan at his house. Drive over, he probably isn't answering his cell much."

Kristen disconnected and shook her head. Well,

word seemed to have spread, and everyone *did* think she would hook up. No wonder she always avoided town like the plague. Well, they would just have to get over it. She wasn't a skank to hop straight into someone else's bed after a breakup. Damn people anyway. But she clearly needed to set the record straight with Nolan. The town would find out the truth within a matter of hours if she knew Michelle, and she did know her. In fact, they might all know before she even got to Nolan's house. She would unpack and bring everything in later. But first, she had a man to talk to.

Chapter Thirty

KRISTEN THOUGHT ABOUT HOW little people knew her as she drove the short distance to Nolan's. Was it her fault, for living such a solitary life up on the mountain? Didn't they realize she lived alone? Without a man in her life—just her and her dog. Why would they think she needed to jump straight into a new affair when she could count on one hand the number of relationships she had ever been in? People were very, very odd—she didn't think she would ever understand them.

Kristen parked in Nolan's driveway, behind his truck, so at least she knew he was home. She went up to the door and rang the bell and waited nervously for him to answer. When he didn't, she rang the bell again and looked in the windows. No sign of anyone. Maybe in the back yard. She went around the side of the house and saw the hugest pile of split wood she'd ever seen, and laughed. *How much wood does he think he's going to need here in town?* She wouldn't use that much at her house on the mountain for two winters. *Silly man.*

But, he wasn't back there either—although she did think she heard music coming from the work shed. Maybe he was in there. She went over to it and looked in the window. There he was—and she couldn't believe her eyes because he was working on a glass sculpture that was magnificent. She just stood there watching, marveling at both the way he moved and how stunning the piece was. It felt almost erotic and fierce at the same time.

Slowly Nolan turned his head and saw her at the window. He jerked his head as if to welcome her inside and she nodded and reached for the door. She walked into light and heat and music.

"Turn the music down, I can't let go of this for another ninety seconds." He looked toward the speakers his iPhone was attached to. No wonder he wasn't answering his phone much.

She turned the sound down and went over nearer to him—not too close to the blazing hot sculpture that she would get burned, but close enough to feel the heat radiating off it. "It's amazing."

He looked her in the eye and said, "It's you... or how I feel about you. You're the inspiration, anyway."

Her breath caught, and she couldn't speak for a moment.

"Maybe you've moved on, but—"

"No, I haven't moved on. The gem cutter in Alamosa is a female. Samantha."

Nolan smiled. "I didn't really believe you'd hook up with someone else that quick. I was surprised when everyone thought you would. They don't know you very well, do they?"

"How much longer do you have to hold that?"

"Done," he said as he turned and set down the tools and removed the heavy gloves.

He moved away from his art, and she walked into his arms. "You know me better than anyone in this town, including my sister."

"That's because I love you. I'm so sorry I was an ass and freaked out over that nightmare."

"Nightmare?"

"Yeah, I've had it for years. It's always been about my sister, but that morning I left, you were the one being raped."

"Oh, Nolan. No wonder you were so upset."

"I don't think I could bear it if someone hurt you like that."

Kristen kissed his cheek. "I'm fine. And I know how to defend myself. And I have Farley."

"Yeah. As long as we can keep him out of the mushrooms."

"Well, with Ted out of the picture, I doubt he'll be getting any more served to him. You need to tell me about what happened with Ted."

"I'll do that right after I kiss you for an hour or two.

I missed you while you were gone." Nolan pulled her in tighter, practically squeezing the breath out of her. But she didn't mind at all.

"I missed you while I was gone too. And I've decided not to go back to my house on the mountain. I'm going to stay in town. I kinda like being around people, even if they don't know me very well."

"We can keep your house up there for our private getaway."

"Our?"

"Well, you *are* going to marry me, aren't you?"

Kristen laughed. "Are you asking?"

"Hell yes, and I'm not letting you get away until you say yes. I have handcuffs, you know. And I know how to use them. So, will you marry me?"

"Yes, I believe I *will* marry you. And maybe I'll use those handcuffs on you."

"Okay."

The End

Coming soon, Mary Ann and Trey's story

Fire on the Mountain

Turn the page for a sneak peek.

Chapter One

"TREY, GET OVER TO THAT house on the ridge and find out why the hell they haven't evacuated. Do they not see the forty-foot flames?"

"Yes, sir," Trey saluted his captain as he hot-footed it out of the forest and across the road. The wind had turned overnight, and more dry lightning strikes had started other patches of fire which merged with the main one—and now the whole damn mountain was on fire. The police were supposed to be evacuating, but it seemed like Trey was moonlighting as police rather than a hotshot wildland fire fighter. Oh, well. Whatever it took.

He ran into the yard and saw a woman pulling the cop—which had come to evacuate her—toward a shed. He ran up to the pair. "We've got to get this place evacuated *now*."

"Oh, two. Hallelujah!" the woman said and grabbed hold of his arm and started towing them both toward the building.

Trey said, "Ma'am, just what's in the shed that's so important to risk your life over?"

"I'm Kristen. The tanks."

The cop said, "But you told me they were loaded."

"The household tanks, yes"—she shoved both of them through the door to the shed—"but not those."

"Oh, shit," he said, a whole bunch of the big tanks—probably acetylene—were standing next to the door.

"I can't move them by myself or even with Mary Ann. They're too heavy," she said pointing to the other woman in the room.

Trey looked at the woman she pointed to. She was a knockout, even all disheveled and dirty from loading up the truck and trying to move the tanks. He touched his mic and said, "Chief, this is Trey at the house on the ridge. I need another couple of guys over here stat and have them bring at least two fire blankets."

"I was just sending them out. Is this an emergency?"

"The biggest one we've got right now. I'll explain later."

He and the cop started carrying out the tanks and laying them in the cradles in the bed of the truck, parked near the shed. Two of his crew ran into the yard and over to the shed.

When they looked inside, Jeff said, "Oh, fuck. Over a half dozen A5s."

At the same time George said, "Thank you, God, for

this woman refusing to leave these behind." All four worked quickly loading the tanks into the truck and securing them in the cradles.

Some other men from town showed up and started hauling out other equipment to put into their truck. He went over to the blond bombshell. "I'm Trey. It's not safe for a pretty lady like you on this mountain."

"I know, but I couldn't just leave Kristen up here to fend for herself. So, I came up to help. I'm Mary Ann." She held out her hand.

He pulled off his glove and took her soft hand in his. "Well, Mary Ann, that's very kind of you, but now that she's got help, you should head down to safety. We don't want anything to happen to you. That would make me sad."

Mary Ann blushed. "I'll get going. Look me up if you get a break. Mary Ann Thompson."

"Will do. I'll buy you a beer or glass of wine—or whatever—as thanks for not leaving us to blow up when those tanks got hot."

"Blown up fire jumpers are not nearly as nice as whole ones."

"Oh, we're hotshots, fire jumpers are a little different.

"Good to know, you can tell me all about it—if you get some free time." She winked at him and went out into the chaos of the yard.

He dearly wished they were not in the middle of an inferno—he would like to get to know her better, much better.